12-10

Dear Reader,

Welcome to *Unlikely Duet, Caledonia Chronicles—Part 1,* another tale in the series of *Great Lakes Romances,* historical fiction full of love and adventure set in bygone days in the region known as Great Lakes Country.

Like the other books in this series, *Unlikely Duet* relays the excitement and thrills of a tale skillfully told, but contains no explicit sex, offensive language, or gratuitous violence.

We invite you to tell us what you would like most to read about in *Great Lakes Romances.* For your convenience, we have included a survey form at the back of the book. Please fill it out and send it to us.

At the back, you will also find descriptions of other romances in this series, and a biography in the *Bigwater Classics* series, stories that will sweep you away to an era of gentility and enchantment, and places of unparalleled beauty and wonder!

Thank you for being a part of *Great Lakes Romances!*

Sincerely,
The Publishers

P.S. Author Donna Winters loves to hear from her readers. You can write her at P.O. Box 177, Caledonia, MI 49316.

ACKNOWLEDGEMENTS

I would like to thank the following for their contributions to this fictional endeavor:

Mary Huggard for expediting delivery of microfilm of the *Caledonia News*

Liz Finkbeiner for loaning her collection of historical data on Caledonia

Andi Parbel for giving me a grand tour of the home in which my fictional heroine lives

Ken Gackler, Mr. History of Caledonia, who spent hours assisting me with historical facts and photos

NOTE

Photos of the home shown on the cover, and the historic churches shown in the back matter of this book are courtesy of the Caledonia Historical Society.

Unlikely Duet

Caledonia Chronicles
Part 1

Donna Winters

Great Lakes Romances®

Bigwater Publishing
Caledonia, Michigan

Unlikely Duet, Caledonia Chronicles Part 1
Copyright c 1998 by Donna Winters

Cover photo of historic home and back matter photos of historic churches are courtesy
    of the Caledonia Historical Society.

Great Lakes Romances is a registered trademark of Bigwater Publishing,
P.O. Box 177, Caledonia, Michigan 49316.

Library of Congress Catalog Card Number: 97-77934
ISBN 0-923048-86-3

Edited by Pamela Quint Chambers
Cover design by Tammy Johnson

Printed in the United States of America

98 99 00   01 02   03   04   /   / 10 9 8 7 6 5 4 3 2 1

CHAPTER

1

Caledonia, Michigan
June 15, 1905

"Caroline!"

Joshua Bolden hurried down the steps of the four-room, yellow brick school at the east end of Center Street into the bright sunshine, determined to speak with his vivacious, dark-haired classmate before she headed home from school. The news he'd been planning to share during two recesses and a lunch hour could wait no longer.

But when her gaze met his, her delicate features, upswept curls, and the vitality in her brown eyes put a hold on that thought. Taking a deep breath, he fingered the tattered ace of diamonds in his pocket--his good-luck charm—and managed to loose his tongue. Quiet words tumbled out.

"Caroline, I can't play in your recital Saturday night."

Caroline Chappell studied the fresh-faced president of their senior class, the best trumpet player in the Caledonia

1

Band. She had planned this recital since childhood—a program in which she would perform as a soloist on the piano and organ, and in a duet for two unaccompanied trumpets with Joshua—a program designed to launch her career as a private music instructor.

Lord, I hope my ears are playing tricks on me, she prayed, nervously twisting the gold and garnet baby ring on her little finger. Swallowing the orange gumdrop she'd been chewing, she grinned. "What kind of a judy do you take me for? Surely, you're joshing me, Joshua—no pun intended."

How he wished he *were* joking. He had practiced the piece, one Caroline had composed, for the past six months, and he wanted desperately to perform it with her. But circumstances were beyond his control.

He ran a hand through his fawn-colored hair. "Afraid I'm serious. Mr. Cavanaugh hired the band to play at seven o'clock Saturday night in front of his hotel. I have to be there, or Professor Neron will throw me out."

"Mr. Cavanaugh hired . . . what could he possibly need the band for?" she asked, unbelieving.

"A balloon ascension," Joshua mumbled.

"A balloon ascension? Well that's a fine thing! Deserting me at the last minute for such nonsense!"

Joshua made no reply. Caroline Chappell was the most talented and dedicated musician he'd ever known, perhaps the finest in the town's history. He couldn't blame her for considering a balloon ascension pure folly.

A moment later, she forced a smile, her tone patronizing. "That's all right, Joshua. You just go and play with the band. No one will even miss you at my recital, least of all, me . . . you *traitor!*"

2

Her words stung, but as she whirled away, angry strides carrying her across School Court and down Center Street, Joshua restrained himself from chasing after her.

Caroline swiftly passed the Henderson place--the brown, two-story house that faced the school from a hill--and the tiny little Davis place in the hollow behind it. She waved to Mrs. Williams, out on her porch, hurried past the Bergys', and crossed West Street. She was beyond Dr. Graybiel's home and office before Deborah Dapprich, her cousin from Detroit who was now a permanent member of the Chappell household, caught up with her.

"Where are you headed in . . . such a rush?" her blond relation asked, struggling to catch her breath as she strained to keep up.

"The Caledonia Hotel," Caroline stated, her steps never slowing as she crossed the Michigan Central Railroad tracks.

"But, whatever for?"

"You'll see!"

While Deborah babbled on about a fanciful butterfly she was planning to embroider on her newest handkerchief, Caroline kept to her silence, and her pace. Assessing the impossible circumstances facing her, she prayed for the right words to say to Mr. Cavanaugh. Passing Bolden & Sons Hardware and Furniture, and Charles Kinsey's general store where straw hats and parasols were on sale in the front window, Caroline hurried by Mr. Beeler's drug store and the VanAmburg sisters' grocery to her destination. Swinging the hotel door wide open, she marched across the uncarpeted lobby. Oblivious to the young man who was in the process of registering, she addressed the silk-suited

3

hotelier with as much politeness as she could muster.

"Mr. Cavanaugh, do you realize the trouble you've caused?"

A grin appeared beneath his waxed mustache. "Miss Chappell, to what do I owe—"

Caroline pressed on. "Perhaps you don't give a hoot in heaven about classical music, but there are *some* of us in Caledonia who *do*."

"Trouble? Classical music? I—"

Temper getting the best of her, she rushed on. "I hope you're happy, Mr. Cavanaugh, because you're about to ruin my recital. *Ruin it!* And after ten years of preparation!"

"But—"

"How in the name of Chopin do you expect anyone to hear the delicate phrases of his *Butterfly* etude when thirty members of a brass band are blaring *Semper Fidelis* with all the air their lungs can hold, and practically in front of the church door?"

She felt a hand at her elbow, and for the first time noticed the narrow-faced fellow beside her. "When is your recital, Miss Chappell? I'd like to hear it?" he asked in velvety tones.

Caroline offered him a blank stare, wondering when he'd come in, where he'd come from, and how he knew her name.

Deborah spoke up. "My cousin's recital is Saturday evening at seven o'clock in the Methodist Episcopal Church across the street, Mr. . . . ?"

"Taman. Neal Taman."

Understanding coming at last, the hotelier spoke again. "So it's the balloon ascension that's caused all this rancor. Perhaps you can reschedule your recital, Miss Chappell."

4

"Impossible!" she snapped, breaking contact with Taman.

"But I'd be glad to pay the cost of the newspaper announcement."

"Too late!" Caroline insisted. "Invitations were mailed out a month ago. The recital is only two days away! Why don't *you* change the date of the balloon ascension?" she asked, finger pointing.

"Impossible," he claimed with ire to match hers. "This Saturday night is the only opening the pilot had in his schedule. Sunday, he'll be off to Chicago to attempt a crossing of Lake Michigan, and on to parts East after that."

Neal Taman's hand again at Caroline's elbow, he turned her to face him. Enthralled by the beauty of her fine features and captivated by her tenacious spirit, he nevertheless addressed her current dilemma. "I think I know of a way to make both you and Mr. Cavanaugh happy."

Deborah, fingering the butterfly pin she always wore on her bodice, asked sweetly, "And what suggestion would you have, Mr. Taman? I—we're all quite eager to hear it."

CHAPTER

2

Joshua stepped past the spools of mechanics wire in the back room of Bolden & Sons Furniture and Hardware, slumped down on a keg of ten-penny nails, and stared at the chest in front of him that bore the faint odor of lemon oil. The family heirloom sure looked spiffy compared to the scarred oak and pine box he'd started refinishing three months ago. Gone were the faded red, mulberry, and black stains. Running his hand over the fancy vine carved into the front oak panel, he admired the burnt orange stain he'd rubbed into it, and the initials, J.B., above.

If great-grandfather Johann Bolden were still alive, he'd have probably objected to the new color, same as his mama, papa, and older brother Zimri did. Joshua didn't care. Fact was, Caroline had a fetish for orange. He first learned about it at the start of the school year when she'd convinced the senior class to adopt it as one of their class colors. Then he was reminded of it again six months ago when they'd started practicing her trumpet duet together. That's when he noticed that the embroideries on her handkerchiefs were orange. So were the tassels on her parasols and the ribbons on her hat. Her flashes of orange and tunes pretty as a songbird's reminded him of a Baltimore oriole.

Even her favorite foods were orange-flavored. Filled layer cakes, puddings, orange gum drops—*especially* orange gum drops which she'd pick one by one out of the jar at Kinsey's general store. And her personality was akin to a fine orange sauce, sweet yet spicy with a dash of cinnamon.

Joshua's thoughts came back to the old chest. He wondered if it would make a proper betrothal gift. It was plain. Maybe too plain now that the Chappells had moved into that big, new place on Railroad Street, with its crenelated tower, sweeping porch, and two-story bays fitted with bowed glass windows on either end of the house. He'd been there many times, but never farther than the music room. Suppose Caroline already had a fancy hope chest tucked away in some corner of the sprawling mansion? He chuckled. He hadn't even begun to court her yet. First came her recital, then graduation, then courtship, the way he figured.

He slid his hand across the pine lid of his chest, smooth as marble, then lifted it a few inches. The essence of the new cedar lining he had fitted to the interior filled his nostrils, just as hopes and dreams of a future with Caroline filled his heart.

Lowering the lid, he thought back. One cold, wintry, Friday afternoon she'd come by the store after school and handed him the music for the duet. "It was written to make the most of your talents," she'd said, her dark eyes beaming with enthusiasm. "You have an excellent range and superb technique." She pointed out the cadenza that soared to high C, adding, "You've simply got to perform it at my recital this spring!"

When he'd looked it over for a few seconds, she said,

"Be at my house Sunday at four for the first rehearsal." Not waiting for a response, she ducked out the door. He hadn't even had a chance to ask who would be playing the second part. One of the other fellows in the band, he assumed, till he got to the Chappells' music room. There was Caroline, trumpet in hand.

He knew she was good at the piano. He'd heard her play in school. And he'd heard her on the organ at church when Mrs. Barber wasn't there. But he couldn't believe she knew how to play the trumpet.

This is the most unlikely duet I ever could've imagined, he thought.

Until she put her horn to her lips. Out came the sweetest sound he'd ever heard from a brass instrument, clear as a skylark's greeting.

They practiced together. Right off, he liked the way they sounded. She wasn't as good as he was on the trumpet—not technically—but she sure was a first-rate musician. Her keen sense of interpretation made him a better player.

Before he knew it, he'd fallen in love with her. Her gay laughter, quick wit, diverse musical talent, and even her darker moods when she fretted that she'd never be ready in time for her spring recital touched his heart and made him care in a way he hadn't anticipated. Many a day during practice in the Chappells' music room, he'd been a sixteenth note away from kissing her pretty, heart-shaped lips. Then he'd take a bar's rest, get control of himself, and concentrate harder than ever on the music in front of him.

Now all those practices were for naught. The recital was out of the question, and maybe the courtship, too. He had to perform with the band. All his friends—including his card-playing pal, Solon—were in the band. They were

8

counting on him. He'd been a loyal member for four years and he couldn't turn his back on them now, could he?

After dinner and studies, Joshua led the way to the dusty second floor above Bolden & Sons Hardware, his brother, Zimri, and their friend, Solon, close behind. He pulled the string on the bare bulb hanging from the center of the ceiling; dim light spilled down on the card table below which was strewn with nuts, bolts, and washers used to keep track of scores. Chairs scraped the unfinished wooden floor as each took his place, claimed his fair share of the hardware, then cut the deck of cards that had been stripped of everything lower than seven for skat, a complicated game requiring as much skill as luck.

The deal fell to Zimri, who passed out batches of three cards all around. Placing two cards face down on the table—the skat cards—he continued to deal the remainder of the deck, first in batches of four, then in batches of three.

Joshua studied his hand. It was heavy in diamonds, somehow reminding him of Grandpa Bolden, who'd taught him and Zimri how to play skat. They'd passed many a rainy afternoon at the game. The memory made Joshua smile. Grandpa Bolden didn't have much. And most of what he *did* have was from his own papa—the old chest, his love of skat, and his good-luck charm—the battered ace of diamonds. But he wasn't poor. Not really. He loved life. He loved his family. And he always had a kind word to share.

Reminiscences aside, Joshua concentrated on the bidding, winning the right to name the version of skat they would play—in this case, *solo*, because his hand was so heavy in one particular suit.

With diamonds as trump, Joshua racked up several points. But his luck didn't hold. He couldn't keep his mind on the game. Thoughts of Caroline and her recital distracted him. At the end of the first session, Zimri, a year older and more experienced at the game, was in the lead. Solon, who'd caught on quickly to the skat rules a couple of years back, was next highest scorer. And Joshua was way behind.

While Solon shuffled to begin the next session, Zimri pulled a newspaper clipping from his pocket. "Almost forgot, Mr. Finkbeiner came into the store today." He named one of Grandpa Bolden's old cronies. "He gave me this article from the *Detroit Free Press*." Opening it, he began to read. "'Skat Players Wanted. The American Skat League will hold its annual tournament at the Cadillac Hotel on Saturday and Sunday, July 1 & 2. Play will be according to the official League rules. The five highest scorers at the end of two days' play will each win a brand new automobile contributed by the city's foremost manufacturers of horseless carriages. Registration for the tournament will take place on Saturday morning at nine in the lobby of the hotel.'"

Joshua imagined himself pulling into Chappells' huge circular drive in a brand new automobile. Caroline 'd be impressed. He'd own the only horseless carriage in town. Or perhaps he'd sell the vehicle and put aside the money for the future. Then reality set in. Riding the Michigan Central all the way to Detroit and staying at the Cadillac Hotel would cost a pretty penny. He couldn't afford to dig into his savings for such a risky venture. Could he?

Zimri jostled his shoulder. "Hey, Josh, you look like you're a million miles away. Or are you figurin' how you'll win that tourney?"

Joshua shook his head. "Can't go. Detroit's a long way from here. It'd cost better than eight bucks just for the round trip ticket!"

Setting the shuffled deck on the table, Solon said, "Maybe it will be in Grand Rapids next year. Then we can all go."

Joshua made no reply. Despite his poor showing in the game tonight, he knew he was better than most at skat. But he wouldn't be going to any tournament to prove it—not this year, anyway.

Weary from a night of lost sleep, Joshua sent his friend, Solon, on to school without him the next morning, then waited at the corner of Johnson and Railroad Streets for Caroline and Deborah to appear. The skat game forgotten as soon as it ended, his thoughts had been dominated by his problem with Caroline. He never should've tried to back out of the recital. He knew that now. He'd hunted the rest of the night for the right words to make an apology.

Shading his eyes from the glare of the early morning sun, he caught sight of Caroline and Deborah coming up the street. But who was the tall, sandy-haired fellow with them? Heading toward the threesome, Joshua jammed his hand into his pants pocket and nervously fingered the ace of diamonds, hoping for good luck.

CHAPTER

3

The closer Caroline came, the more Joshua worried. The stranger with her and her cousin sure was making a hit. Caroline's laugh, rhythmic and repetitive like a woodpecker in stitches, dominated the quieter, bubblier sound of her cousin's giggle. When only a few feet separated Joshua from them, the joyous noise evaporated, Caroline's animated expression turning placid.

"Caroline, may I have a word with you, please?"

She offered a subtle smile, glad to run into him. "Certainly, Joshua."

With a fleeting glance at the others, he asked, "May we speak in private?"

She sent her friends on without her, grateful for the opportunity to share news of her own that was certain to please him.

Joshua drew a breath, his words rushing out. "I'm sorry about yesterday. I still want to play in your recital, if you'll let me."

Her smile broadened. Putting aside the foremost thoughts on her mind, she commented on his apology instead. "Before, you said you couldn't, that the band performance—"

"I know what I said. I was wrong. I promised you last

winter that I'd play the duet in your recital, and that's what I'm gonna do."

"But Professor Neron throws out any band member who misses a performance," she reminded him.

"Then maybe it's time I quit the band."

Caroline's heart leaped. "Would you really do that for me—for the sake of my recital?"

He nodded.

She wanted to throw her arms about Joshua's neck and kiss him soundly on the cheek. Instead, she offered a wide smile. "Joshua Bolden, I have the most wonderful news for you!"

He waited expectantly.

She opened her mouth, but no words came out. Instead, laughter began pianissimo and grew to a fortissimo staccato that made him laugh, too. Soon, the two of them were consumed, yet he didn't know why, only that her ebullience cast a net around him that drew him in and lifted his spirits.

"Joshua . . . " she struggled to control her mirth. "The band . . . my recital . . . " Despite her efforts, she slipped into laughter again.

This time, he didn't laugh with her, only stood amused, watching and listening, offering his handkerchief when happy tears dampened her silky complexion.

She dabbed the moisture away. Determined to control herself, she considered a better approach to the knowledge she would share and prefaced it softly. "Joshua, I'm highly honored that you would give up the band in order to play in my recital. I'd be a blind judy not to realize it's the nicest thing that ever happened to me!"

She stood beaming at him, her face lit with a joy that made the June sunshine seem dull. He ached to share the

13

depths of his feelings for her, but now wasn't the time. "What's your news?" he gently prodded.

"You don't have to give up the band!" she replied brightly. Starting up the hill toward school, she returned his handkerchief, mildly scented with a hint of the orange blossom toilet water she always wore, and explained the change in circumstances. "Mr. Cavanaugh has postponed the balloon ascension until my recital is finished. You can play with me first, then with the band!"

"But what about the reception your mama was gonna give after the recital? It'd be impolite of me—"

"Canceled. I talked her into giving a dinner for the graduating class next Thursday, instead. Here's your invitation."

As he studied his name, written in brown calligraphy on the pale orange envelope, he pondered the news of the postponement. His apology had been for naught, his sleeplessness a waste. But he was glad he'd revealed his loyalty to Caroline. At least he'd made one small step toward declaring the full measure of his devotion to her. He slid the invitation into his pocket alongside his ace of diamonds, then fingered the tattered playing card once again, convinced it had changed his luck from faulty to flawless.

The final rehearsal for the recital was already under way when Neal Taman slipped into a back pew of the Methodist Episcopal Church to listen to the rapid organ strains of Bach's *Toccata and Fugue in D minor*. He knew in an instant that Caroline Chappell was a country mile ahead of most young ladies her age where musical talent was concerned. She was precocious and persistent, too, getting under his skin the first moment he'd seen her. But

14

she wasn't what he was looking for. Not now, anyway.

He redirected his attention to the young lady in the front pew who was listening with obvious admiration. He'd suspected from the instant he'd met Deborah Dapprich that she would suit his purposes quite well. Beneath the butterfly pin on her blouse and the modest bustle under her skirt lay attractive, womanly curves. And the blond pouf atop her head further enhanced her outward appeal.

The fugue ended and Deborah rose from her place beside an older woman—a music teacher, he presumed—to stand front and center of the empty choir loft. Caroline, at the piano now, played several bars of introduction laden with Baroque trills, then Deborah opened her mouth to sing. Taman listened in amazement to her light soprano voice rendering an air from Handel's *Messiah*. "If God Be For Us" had never sounded better.

His heart went into a trill of its own. The girl was a more perfect fit for his needs than he'd guessed. Not only did she embody the physical qualities so important in the line of work he had in mind for her, she could sing like an angel as well. Her vocal talent would be a welcome asset.

And he was fully aware that she was singing to impress him. Her gaze never left him throughout her song, then wavered only seconds when she finished her piece and positioned herself between Caroline and the young man he'd seen earlier that day to turn pages during their trumpet duet. Rehearsal over, he waited for the older woman who'd been advising them to take her leave, then went forward to speak with them.

"Congratulations! You'll be putting on quite a classical performance tomorrow night!" His gaze briefly took in all three musicians, settling on Deborah who was first to respond.

"Thank you, Mr. Taman! When I invited you to come hear us this afternoon, I wasn't really sure . . . " She fidgeted with the wing of her enamel butterfly pin.

"I'd show up?" he asked. At her nod and smile, he continued. "It's been my pleasure to hear you all perform. Now, if you'll allow me, I'd like to treat the three of you to lemonade at the hotel."

Deborah and Caroline spoke almost at once.

"We'd love to!"

"No, thank you."

Caroline continued. "We're expected home immediately after rehearsal. We need our rest for the performance tomorrow."

Deborah shrugged. "She's right. But you may walk me home, if you wish."

Taman caught the look of disapproval on Caroline's face as Deborah linked her arm with his and headed toward the door.

Her cousin and Taman gone, Caroline turned to Joshua. "I don't know what it is about that man, but I just don't trust him."

Opening his case to put away his trumpet, Joshua replied, "I was surprised to see him walking you and Deborah to school."

"He just sort of showed up when we left the house this morning. I suppose there isn't much to occupy his time in Caledonia."

Joshua latched his own case, then Caroline's. "Did you say he's here to rest?"

Collecting music from the music stands and the piano rack, Caroline recalled what little she and Deborah had learned about Taman after their encounter with him the previous afternoon. "He's a banker's son recovering from fatigue. At least that's what he said when he insisted on walking us home from the hotel yesterday afternoon."

Joshua reached for the handle of his case, tucking Caroline's under his arm. "Odd. He doesn't look tired."

"My thoughts exactly." Slipping the music into her portfolio, she preceded Joshua down the aisle, switching off lights on the way out the church door.

The evening sky over the west end of Center Street had taken on the hue of orange sherbet. A soft, summer breeze tinged with an equine essence teased the curls on Caroline's forehead, whispering through the leaves of a nearby maple as resident robins sang tribute to a dying day. Peacefulness reigned on Lake Street and Railroad Street as well, where the Chappells' big white house dominated the landscape.

From the sweeping front porch, Joshua could see Deborah and Taman on a bench in the garden, engrossed in conversation. Caroline cast a disapproving glance their way before turning to face him.

"Rehearsal went well tonight." She reached for her trumpet case, her gaze turning troubled as she again focused on the couple in the garden. "Deborah never sang better, but the way she's talking Mr. Taman's ear off, she won't have a voice left by tomorrow."

Not wanting Caroline to fret on the eve of her recital, Joshua said, "I'll invite Taman to walk back to Center Street with me, if you like."

After a moment's thought, Caroline shook her head. "I haven't seen my cousin this happy since she moved in with us two months ago. I'll give her a few more minutes with

17

him, then I'll drag her off to bed myself, if I have to. Good night, Joshua." Her gaze rested momentarily on the set of his mouth, the trumpet embouchure she had admired for months, and for the briefest instant she wondered how it would lend itself to a kiss.

Joshua's desire to press a good-night kiss on Caroline's heart-shaped lips was nearly overwhelming, but he restrained himself knowing full well the time for such affections lay far in the future. "Good night, Caroline. See you tomorrow night." He bound off the porch, eager to put a safe distance between them lest his longing became cause for regret.

Caroline watched Joshua's sturdy, athletic form cross the railroad tracks and head up Lake Street, then she went indoors. Setting horn and music aside, she passed by the bronze lamp fashioned in the shape of Pocahontas and climbed the spiral oak staircase.

The door to the master bedroom stood open, and Caroline instinctively headed there, her mother's voice greeting her even before she arrived.

"Caroline, how did your rehearsal go?"

She entered the spacious, oak-trimmed room with its chintz wallpaper and frieze of red roses. The faint scent of her mother's rose potpourri welcomed her. She paused at the bowl of dried petals to inhale deeply before joining her mother at the side window where she was gazing out at the garden below. "Rehearsal went well. Deborah was in especially fine voice!"

"For the sake of Mr. Taman, I assume. Why, this very minute, she's sitting so close to the fellow, she could count every hair on his chinny-chin-chin if she so desired!"

Caroline laughed. Ottilia joined her, their voices like a

duet of tickled woodpeckers.

But the laughter died quickly, Ottilia's expression sobering. "Caroline, whatever am I going to do about your cousin? She was trouble as a small child, and she's trouble still—pilfering from VanAmburgs' Grocery when she first arrived, neglecting her studies. She has you to thank for getting her through the school year."

Caroline recalled childhood days when Deborah would come to stay for weeks at a time. Together, they'd made mischief, but nothing as serious as the total neglect of studies Deborah had fallen into as a high school student. For the past several weeks, Caroline had spent long hours preparing her cousin for each day's lessons, and the effort had paid off. At least Deborah had brought her grades up to passing in every subject.

Scowling at the couple in the garden, her mother continued. "Now, Deborah's acting like . . . like . . . "

"A siren determined to lure an unsuspecting sailor."

"Your description is charitable—and a tad naïve. Mr. Taman is far from unsuspecting."

"I suppose you're right," Caroline admitted. Turning from the garden scene, she faced her mother. "Deborah's faults aside, you have to admit she's thrown herself wholeheartedly into her voice lessons. Mrs. Barber, at least, speaks very highly of her."

"Deborah *does* have her fair share of the musical talent so prevalent in the Overton side of the family." Ottilia conceded, pacing to her vanity. "But I could just throttle that sister of mine—may she rest in peace—for raising such a nuisance of a child. She should have paid closer attention to the girl rather than roaming about the country like a gypsy, performing in those bawdy houses."

"A sad waste of talent, considering Aunt Emeline sang every bit as beautifully as Jenny Lind."

"Emiline always was the black sheep of the family. It's not at all surprising that she died . . . never mind."

Caroline knew all about the way in which her aunt had died. Deborah had explained the unsavory circumstances in full detail.

Ottilia returned to the window. With a heavy sigh, she said, "Deborah has thrown herself at that Mr. Taman quite enough for one night. I shall simply have to go down there and—"

"I'll go get her, Mother," Caroline offered. Her gaze falling on the photograph of her father framed in silver on the vanity, she paused to ask, "By the way, is Papa home yet?"

Ottilia shook her head. "He's working late in the city, as usual."

"The Sutherland case?" Caroline asked, referring to the trial which had been monopolizing her father and his Grand Rapids law practice for the past several weeks.

"None other. He'll likely stay overnight again."

"He'll be home in time for my recital tomorrow night, won't he?"

Ottilia nodded. "He'll be home for dinner. Parker and Roxana will be here too—they'll stay the weekend." She named Caroline's older brother and his wife. Turning from the window, she pulled two tickets from beneath the mirror on her vanity and held them up. "Do you know what these are?"

Caroline shook her head.

Ottilia smiled. "They're two tickets to the Summer Reception next Saturday night. It's been months since your father has taken me anywhere but to church. After your graduation dinner next Thursday, and your commencement on Friday, we're going to have a night to ourselves." She slid the tickets between the glass and frame of her husband's portrait, one of a grouping of photographs by Mr. Kinsey, the village photographer.

"Papa will be sure to see them there," Caroline commented, pausing to admire the recent photographs of Deborah and herself which flanked her father's.

"And every time I look at his picture this week, I'll think of the good time we're going to have next Saturday," Ottilia observed. "In fact, I think I'll even go to Grand Rapids next week and buy myself a new dress!"

"You do that, Mother!" Caroline encouraged.

As she headed downstairs, the portrait image of her father remained in her mind—his broad frame, square jaw, and full, dark head of hair. It dawned on her that he'd been spending so much time away from home in recent weeks that she couldn't have missed him more if he'd taken a two-month European holiday.

Such thoughts were pushed aside by the sound of Deborah's gay laughter as Caroline approached the white iron bench in the garden where her cousin sat at an angle, knee to knee with Taman.

Deborah rose the moment she saw her cousin. "Caroline, I have the best news! You aren't going to believe what Mr. Taman just asked me!"

CHAPTER

4

Taman stood beside Deborah, his mouth curved in a smile bereft of warmth as he faced Caroline. "If your folks are available, we'd like to speak with them—and you, of course."

"Papa isn't home, but Mother is in her room. I'll ask her to come down to the parlor." Leading them inside, she prayed her cousin hadn't formed an instant romantic attachment to the Caledonia newcomer.

Within minutes, the four of them were seated in the front parlor; Deborah a tad too close to Taman for propriety on the peach velvet sofa, Caroline on the matching balloon-back chair opposite the couple, and her mother on the ivory brocade love seat. The tapestry carpet seemed to reflect the diversity of the ensemble gathered upon it, Caroline mused, its white background and pastel flowers a reflection of the bright look on Deborah's face; its black border shadowing the doubt in Ottilia's uneasy smile.

Ottilia spoke first. "I understand you have some news for us."

Deborah's gaze shifted from the fellow beside her to

her aunt. "A week from tonight, just as soon as I've gradu-ated high school, I'm leaving with Mr. Taman to star in a new musical drama he's staging in Cleveland!"

Caroline gasped.

Ottilia opened her mouth to speak, but Taman cut her off.

"I've been looking a long, long time for the right person to fill the starring role. Your niece is extraordinarily talent-ed, Mrs. Chappell. She's perfect for the part!"

Caroline addressed Taman. "But you told us you were in banking. How can you be in the theater business, too?"

"I'm a banker by day with my father. Evenings, I'm in the theater business with my uncle." He chuckled lightly. "I suppose that's how I got so worn out—burning both ends of the candle."

Ottilia spoke up. "Pardon my saying so, Mr. Taman, but I hardly know you, and here you are, proposing to whisk my niece off to a far-away city and make her into a theatrical star!"

Reaching for his inside pocket, he produced a folded paper and a business card. "My offer is perfectly legiti-mate, Mrs. Chappell. Here's a playbill from last season, and the information concerning my father's bank."

She perused them briefly, returning them to Taman. "Your offer may be legitimate." Her focus shifted to her niece. "But Deborah, I want you to put thoughts of the theater out of your head. I have no intention of allowing you to take up that sort of life."

"Aunt Ottilia, how *could* you?" she cried.

"I won't have you going down the same road as your mother," Ottilia asserted, her voice growing shrill. "You, of all people, should understand that it can only lead to de-

23

struction."

"But—"

Caroline addressed her cousin in earnest. "What about the plans we've been making these last two months for our music academy? You were going to offer singing lessons—we were going to use the music room on alternate days to schedule our students. That's the main purpose of our recital—to let the community know that we're ready to accept students for private instruction!"

"But I want to be on the stage! I want to hear the applause!"

Ottilia shook her head. "I forbid it."

Deborah turned to Neal. "Say something! Make Aunt Ottilia understand that I *must* go with you to star in your musical!"

"Your aunt's concern is understandable," he allowed, "but unnecessary." To Ottilia, he said, "We hire many young ladies from various towns and cities. As one of the benefits of employment, we offer food and lodging in a lovely, chaperoned home where each girl has a room to call her own."

"That's all well and good, but it doesn't change the fact that Deborah would be taking up the life of a stage player."

Deborah grew solemn. "Aunt Ottilia, *please* think it over!"

Jaw set, Ottilia repeated, "I won't have you taking up that sort of life, and that's the last I'll hear of it."

"You're so *unfair!*" Deborah charged, beginning to sob.

Neal offered his handkerchief. "Now, there, Miss Dapprich, please don't cry."

"But . . . but . . . " she stammered.

Neal spoke in placating tones. "No good purpose will

be served in causing a fuss, Miss Dapprich. Your aunt is only doing what she thinks best. Come see me out." Rising, he took her by the elbow, bidding good night to Ottilia and Caroline on his way to the door.

Ottilia stood. "I hope that's the last I'll hear of *that*. I'd better check with Vida one last time about tomorrow's dinner menu."

Caroline rose. "She's going to bake my favorite orange layer cake for dessert, isn't she?"

Ottilia nodded, nudging her daughter toward the stairs. "Off to bed with you, now. You need your rest."

Caroline headed for the staircase, pausing by the window in the front door to observe Taman and her cousin on the veranda. They were standing very close, Taman's hands lightly on her shoulders. He appeared to be speaking in earnest. Deborah listened intently, her sad countenance transforming into a tiny smile. Caroline wished for all the world that she could hear what was being said on the opposite side of the oak door, but no sound penetrated the thick wood and heavy, beveled glass.

Climbing the stairs, she put the couple out of her mind, her thoughts focusing again on the recital to come. She was undressing when she heard her mother come upstairs, Deborah following moments later to knock softly on the master bedroom door.

Caroline quickly pulled on her wrapper, unlatching her own door to hear her cousin speaking in dulcet tones.

"Aunt Ottilia, may I have a word with you, please?" she asked, adding, "Come on out, Caroline, I'd like you to hear this, too."

Moments later, Ottilia opened her door, gazing upon Deborah with suspicion. "If you've come to argue further—"

She shook her head, blond tendrils bouncing. "I've come to apologize. I was wrong to argue with you, Aunt Ottilia. You've given me the finest home I've ever known, and I've behaved shamefully. I'm sorry. Please forgive me."

Ottilia reached for Deborah, pulling her into an embrace. Pressing her cheek against her niece's, she said, "You're forgiven, Deborah. I'm glad you see the wisdom of staying right here in Caledonia." Pulling away, she caressed Deborah's chin. "Now, go on to bed and get your rest. And no more talking until tomorrow. I want to hear you in fine voice at the recital!"

Deborah planted an impetuous kiss on her aunt's cheek. "Good night, Aunt Ottilia!" Slapping her hand over her own mouth, she whispered, "Sorry, I forgot I wasn't supposed to talk!"

With a quarter hour to go before the start of her recital, Caroline checked the valves of her trumpet for the sixth time to make sure they were properly oiled, then returned the instrument to its case which lay open on Pastor Phillips's oak desk. Joshua, evidently calmer than she, had settled into the chair behind the desk. Head bent, eyes closed, hands folded, he appeared to be in prayer. Caroline tried to pray, too, but no words would come.

Pacing a few feet away, she admired the handsome fit of Joshua's summer tweed suit. His long, silk tie and the crisp points on the collar of his white dress shirt matured his youthful look by a year or two, making him even more handsome than she had realized. But the pleasant thought was a fleeting one.

Anxieties concerning their upcoming performance overtook her again. Opening the door of the study but a crack, she peeked out at the sanctuary which was divided by two aisles. Her mother sat alone near the front on the right. Across the aisle, Mrs. Barber, her beloved music teacher and mentor, also sat alone. Halfway to the back sat Joshua's folks and his brother, Zimri. The pew opposite theirs held Caroline's brother and his wife, and in the last row on the right was Neal Taman. At the door beside him stood Deborah, a stack of programs in her hand that, from all appearances, would go to waste.

Disappointment settled bitter and heavy within. Where were the friends and classmates Caroline had played for time and again at school? Where were the aunts, uncles, and cousins from the other side of the county who had received personal invitations written in her very own hand? Most disturbing of all, where was her father? Caroline closed the door. Tears blurring her vision and staining her cheeks, it dawned on her that not even the members of her very own church had come to lend their support.

From across the tiny study, Joshua was about to ask how the audience was filling up, but Caroline's expression said it all. His heart breaking for her, he reached for his handkerchief and rose.

"No need for tears," he said with quiet confidence, "the church 'll fill up. It's still ten minutes till seven." He lifted her chin to dab away the moisture on her cheeks, thinking how comely she looked in her fancy black lace and satin gown. A tad of orange enamel decorated the gold bar pin clasped at the center of her bodice. He couldn't help smiling at the clever way she'd found to wear her favorite color, even on this fancy occasion.

Despite Joshua's gentle smile, confident words and tender touch, anger began rising within Caroline. Taking the handkerchief from him, she blew her nose, crumpled the cotton square into a ball, and threw it into the open horn case on the desk. "How do you know the church will fill up? It looks to me like we'll be playing to about a dozen people!"

"Plenty more will come," he asserted.

She was about to argue the logic of his claim when the door of the study opened to reveal her father, tired and a trifle disheveled with his tie loosened and celluloid collar flapping.

Caroline rushed to greet him. "Papa! I was afraid you'd miss my recital!"

His thick arms opened wide, a smile spreading the width of his broad face. He hugged her tightly, lifting her slightly off the ground. "I wouldn't miss it for the world, Orange Blossom!"

Caroline basked momentarily in his warm embrace, and the comforting essence of vanilla pipe tobacco that lingered on his lapel, then she released herself. "I'm playing every piece for you tonight, Papa, and it will be my best performance ever!"

He chucked her chin. "That's my Orange Blossom! I'll be listening to each note!"

As he slipped out the door, she picked up her horn again and ran through the fingerings of the first few bars of the duet. Returning the instrument to its case, she silently played Bach's *Toccata and Fugue in D minor* on the desktop until Deborah entered the study.

The delicate raspberry ruching on her collar brought out the natural blush in her cheeks. The fit of her pin-tucked bodice, the nip of her narrow waistband, and the bustle-like folds of her organdy overskirt enhanced her natural curves, giving her an attractive and mature appearance that belied her youth. It was no mystery why Taman wanted to hire her.

"It's a few minutes past seven," she announced, fussing with the butterfly pin on her bodice. "I think you should start the recital."

"How many people came?" Caroline asked apprehensively.

After a moment's thought, Deborah replied, "Everyone who counts."

Caroline fiddled nervously with the ring on her little finger. "What a judy I've been, to think I could fill the church at my recital."

Joshua rose from the desk chair. "Don't worry about the size of the audience. Just go out and do your best."

She took a deep breath and opened the door. Shocked by what she saw, she shrank back, quickly closing it again.

CHAPTER

5

Heart a-flutter, Caroline turned to Joshua. "The church is full! Absolutely packed!"

He grinned. "I told you it'd fill up."

"But ... "

Waving a finger at the door, Deborah repeated with a smile, "I think you should start the recital. Professor Neron and the entire Caledonia Band are out there waiting to hear you, along with the rest of the community!"

Opening the door once more, Caroline stepped into the sanctuary to polite applause and seated herself on the organ bench. Pausing to glance at the audience, she saw Pastor Phillips and his wife in the first row along with several faithful church members. Classmates from school filled the third and fourth rows. Aunts, uncles, and cousins from the north end of the county occupied the center section while Professor Neron and members of the Caledonia band filled the back rows and stood along the walls. Even Hugh Cavanaugh had come. Anxiously twisting her ring, she removed it from her finger and set it atop the organ as was her usual custom. Hands poised over the keys, toes lightly touching the pedals, she sounded the opening phrase of the *Toccata and Fugue in D minor.* Almost without conscious thought, her fingers and feet took over, executing every run, seeking out every chord flawlessly to the end of the piece.

When the final note faded away, a deafening silence hung in the air and Caroline was convinced that this audience had no appreciation for her performance, or for Bach. Then applause burst forth, filling the church from narthex to choir loft, from maple floor to high plaster ceiling.

Caroline slid off the organ bench and curtsied, then curtsied twice more before silence reigned again. Proceeding to the piano to perform three Bach inventions, it seemed her fingers could do no wrong. Throughout the first half of her recital, she hit no bad notes, returning to the study for intermission after a hearty round of applause.

Deborah greeted her with a hug. "You're going to have plenty of new students after tonight!"

Joshua nodded, a smile lighting his face. "She's right! You'll be so busy giving piano lessons, you won't have time to play trumpet duets anymore."

His words came as a shock. She'd been so wrapped up in preparation for tonight's performance, she hadn't given thought to the fact that when it was over, she'd no longer need to practice regularly with Joshua. "I . . . I plan to keep on composing for the trumpet," she replied, "solos with accompaniments that only you and I could do justice to." Hoping she hadn't sounded too forward, she focused again on the recital pieces yet to be performed, reminding Deborah, "Three Chopin pieces, then your solo. Will you be ready?"

Deborah ran a scale sotto-voce, then sang the first

phrase of her piece in a clear, full voice.

Caroline nodded approval, telling Joshua, "Don't forget to come out and turn pages for me during her solo."

"You worry too much," he chided. Checking his pocket watch, he said, "Go on, now. It's time."

Pausing to silently perform the opening bars of Chopin's Opus 70, No. 1 on the desk, she confidently entered the sanctuary to polite applause from her audience. It seemed no more than three minutes passed before the waltzes were finished and Deborah appeared, garnering more applause as she took her place front and center, hands clasped in classical pose. Joshua pulled up a chair beside Caroline while she checked the corners of the pages to see that they were curled enough for him to grasp easily. At Deborah's nod, she began the introduction.

Again, her cousin sang like a professional, her soprano voice strong enough to carry to the narthex, her diction so precise each word could be easily understood. When the last note had faded away, Taman led the enthusiastic applause which lasted for a good two minutes. Deborah was absolutely glowing as she returned to the study with Caroline and Joshua to prepare for the final piece, the trumpet duet.

Caroline hugged her cousin. "You've done it, Deborah! You've sung with a voice Caledonia shall never forget!"

"Do you really think so?" she asked, her blue eyes sparkling with satisfaction.

Joshua said, "After that performance, a good number of folk's 'll want to hire you to teach their daughters."

"I . . . ah . . . " Deborah stammered, her radiance fading momentarily. But she recovered quickly, lifting Caroline's trumpet from her case and handing it to her. "You'd better

32

warm up a bit. Your audience is waiting, and they're expecting a grand finale of a trumpet duet!"

Caroline blew into her horn, warming the brass and working her keys, then quietly running some scales. Joshua did the same while Deborah gathered their music. A couple of minutes later, when Caroline's embouchure felt equal to the challenges of the duet, she gathered Joshua and Deborah close.

"Let's pray," she told them, bowing her head. As words came to mind, she felt Joshua's hand enfolding hers, imbuing her with a warmth and confidence that was reflected in her petition. "Heavenly father, you've blessed us greatly here tonight, and we thank you for the joy that fills our hearts. Be with us now as we offer the closing performance. Let us be a blessing to those who have come to listen, and help us to continue using our talents in the way you intended. In Jesus' precious name, Amen."

"Amen," repeated Joshua.

With a squeeze of her hand, he released her. Waiting for her and Deborah to precede him into the sanctuary, he quickly tucked his hand into his pocket, fingering the tattered ace of diamonds for good luck.

Applause sounded the instant the study door opened, dying by the time Deborah had placed their music on the stand. The ensuing silence was so full of expectation, Caroline could feel the electricity in the air.

Exchanging anxious glances with Joshua, they lifted their horns, sounding the opening notes precisely at his signal. The first movement, a short, lilting tune, ran its course without error. Following a brief pause, the second, slower movement began. It afforded a greater depth of feeling, relying more on tone than technique. Again, a pause followed while Deborah turned the page to the third and final movement. In that fleeting moment, Caroline could hear the swift runs and crescendos in her mind, passages written to make the most of Joshua's rapid, precise tonguing, solid upper range, and powerful lungs. Watching for his signal to begin, she read a high degree of anticipation and confidence in his expression. With a bob of his horn, the duet resumed.

Splendidly, his sound soared to the ceiling beams, reverberating and resonating, echoing against itself, and in harmony with the notes Caroline supplied. The result was compelling, driving him onward with such momentum Caroline was afraid for a moment that Joshua would lose the timing in his rush. But he managed to stay in rhythm, taking full advantage of Caroline's accents on the first and third beats of each measure.

Almost too quickly to comprehend, he had reached his cadenza. Slowing momentarily, he held a half note its full two beats and then some, following it with a dozen sixteenth notes. After a three-beat rest, the phrase repeated on higher notes, then repeated twice more, culminating on a high C that lingered for a full measure. When the resolution began, phrase after phrase descended the staff in a flirtatious manner, making a transition into the main refrain where Caroline joined him for the rousing finish.

When the final harmony faded, Professor Neron rose to his feet. "Bravo! Encore!" he shouted, evoking the same responses from the members of his band.

Within moments, the entire audience was on its feet begging for more. Joshua bowed. Caroline curtsied.

Nearly shouting to make himself heard above the applause, he told Caroline, "I think we should play the third movement again."

"Are you up to it?" she asked.

He nodded, raising his horn to begin again. The audience fell silent, reclaiming seats for a repeat performance.

Caroline raised her trumpet, awaiting Joshua's signal to begin. The second performance was as flawless as the first, and a tad bit livelier, becoming even more impressive when Joshua ad libbed the cadenza, embellishing with trills and grace notes, reaching high C and flirting with high E before descending the scale. Again, the audience went wild, applauding even before the finish. Returning with Caroline three times for bows and curtsies, Joshua entered the study for the last time, setting aside his horn and taking Caroline in his arms to swing her around. "We've done it!" he exclaimed. "We've given this town a performance they're gonna be talking about for a good long time!"

Joshua's strong embrace sent Caroline's heart into *tempo allegro*. When he set her on her feet again, she was reluctant to part. Suppressing a powerful desire to hug his neck and kiss his cheek, she absently tried to fiddle with ring on her little finger, only to discover it missing.

As if on cue, Deborah removed it from her own finger. "I noticed it on the organ when I went out to sing my solo. I think it gave me luck."

"Heavens to hogwash!" Caroline exclaimed. "You don't need a piece of jewelry to make you sing well. You've got real talent!" To Joshua, she said, "And so do you! No one could have made my trumpet composition sound any better than you did. I'm going to rewrite the cadenza the way you played it that last time."

He shrugged off the compliment, about to make a reply when her father burst through the study door.

"You did it, Orange Blossom! You gave this town a performance they won't soon forget!" He placed a smacking kiss on her forehead, then hugged her tight. "Now come along, the three of you. Your entire audience is waiting!" He led them down an aisle choked with relatives, friends, schoolmates, church folk, and band members who extended their compliments.

One young lady, a plainly dressed stranger of about thirteen, eagerly introduced herself to Caroline. "Miss Chappell, I'm Tess Johnson. I just wanna say how wonderful you sounded. You sure are talented!" She offered her hand, and was pumping Caroline's rather vigorously as she asked, "How much do you charge for music lessons? I'd sure like to play the pie-anna good as you, some day."

Caroline smiled at the girl's pronunciation of the instrument. "Lessons cost fifty cents apiece. Would you like to sign up?"

Tess released Caroline's hand. "I . . . I'll have to let you know."

Caroline nodded, and moved on. In the narthex, still jammed with supporters, Professor Neron patted Joshua on the shoulder enthusiastically. "Outstanding performance, young man!" To Caroline, he said, "Young lady, my band would consider it a real honor to include you in the ranks. What do you say? Will you join us tonight?"

Caroline released a staccato laugh. "I think not. I need a lot more practice before I can play those Sousa marches you favor." She turned to speak with Mrs. Barber, who had taught and inspired Caroline since age eight when she'd moved to Caledonia, and H.B. Cavanaugh, who lavished her with high praise, while Joshua accepted accolades from his fellow band members.

Minutes later, the narthex was empty of all but Joshua, Caroline, and her father. On the street outside, she could hear the band sounding a rousing rendition of *El Capitan.*

Joshua headed for the study. "I'd better get my horn and get out there."

Caroline was about to collect her own trumpet and music from the study when H.B. Cavanaugh suddenly reappeared, arm extended. "Miss Chappell, in honor of your fine performance, please accept my invitation to be among the first passengers this evening to ascend in Mr. Higley's balloon!"

A refusal was on her lips when her father nudged her toward Cavanaugh. "Great idea, H.B.! My daughter would love to go up!"

"But Papa, my horn and my music—"

He took her aside, speaking confidentially. "Your cousin and Mr. Taman will be going up in the balloon, too. Your mother and I are counting on you to go with them and sort of keep an eye on things. I'll see that your trumpet and music get home."

After a moment's consideration, Caroline forced a smile and returned to the hotelier, placing her arm in his. "Thank you for the invitation, Mr. Cavanaugh. I'd be a real judy to turn you down."

"Now, where's that Bolden fellow?" he asked, glancing back over his shoulder.

With perfect timing, Joshua entered the narthex, trumpet in hand.

"Young man, would you like to join Miss Chappell and some others for a ride in Mr. Higley's balloon?"

"I . . . uh . . . "

"Miss Chappell is going up. She won't take no for your

answer, and if you're worried about Professor Neron, I'll see to it he doesn't dismiss you from the band for missing the first few marches," Cavanaugh claimed, nudging them both out the door.

The moment they appeared on the doorstep, a quartet of classmates rushed forward, and before Caroline knew what was happening, she and Joshua had been lifted onto their shoulders and were being carried toward the balloon amidst the lively notes of Sousa's *High School Cadets* march and the joyful clamor of friends and neighbors.

Never in her wildest dreams had she imagined such an end to their performance. The quiet evening she had envisioned at home with her family was not to be. Instead, she was being thrust into the center of the very spectacle she had planned to avoid—the balloon ascension.

With a quick, silent prayer, she pleaded for God's grace in accepting this unanticipated turn of events—asking Him to make her heart light as the bright purple and yellow balloon suspended in the midst of Center Street half a block away. A minute later, she and Joshua were lowered to the ground beside the open door of the balloon basket which had been decorated with bold purple and yellow stars and stripes. A stocky gentleman wearing a tall purple and yellow striped hat and black tailcoat made a sweeping gesture.

"Welcome aboard the finest balloon this side of Lake Michigan! I'm Mr. Higley, your pilot."

Lifting her skirt, Caroline stepped inside the wicker gondola followed by Joshua.

Taman welcomed them with a smile. "Congratulations, on your performance! Anytime the two of you and Miss Dapprich would like to bring your talents to Cleveland, I'd be happy to arrange a concert date at my uncle's theater."

Deborah's eyes lit with enthusiasm. "Wouldn't that be just the finest thing, the three of us—"

Caroline interrupted. "We won't be coming to Cleveland anytime soon, Mr. Taman." To Deborah, she said, "We need to put all our efforts into our music academy here in Caledonia, remember?"

Deborah lowered her gaze. "You're right, of course."

Having secured the door, Mr. Higley said, "I'm ready to begin the ascent, if you are."

Caroline fought a powerful urge to exit the basket. Exchanging glances with Joshua, she could tell he was feeling the same. But as he reached for her hand, his confident words belied his doubtful look.

"Take her up, Mr. Higley. We're ready!"

Instantly, the pilot raised his megaphone and commanded his crew, "Pay out the line!"

Caroline held tight to Joshua's hand as the windlass began to turn, releasing the tether that allowed the basket to rise while the band struck up *Stars and Stripes Forever*. At first, her stomach felt as if it were still grounded. And on Joshua's face was a pallor that seemed to reflect her own uneasiness. But as the airship ascended, revealing more of the village below, she found herself fascinated with the ever increasing view of the gravity-bound world.

"Joshua, your folks are right down there, in front of your store. See them waving at us?" She shouted to make herself heard above the march music, which seem to rise up in full volume. "And look! There's Zimri, near the windlass!" She prayed the sights would help to take his mind off himself.

Pointing in the direction of Van Amburg's Grocery,

Deborah was equally enthusiastic. "There's Aunt Ottilia, and Uncle Charles. And Cousin Parker and Roxana!" She waved with abandon.

As the basket rose above store rooftops, it caught a westerly breeze and began to rotate, prompting a question from Taman. "Mr. Higley, why is it you use only one tether? I thought even the Civil War balloons used at least three."

Eyes sparkling with interest, the pilot replied in a volume sufficient to be heard above the strains of Sousa. "You're absolutely right! The Union balloonists such as Thaddeus Sobieski Constantine Lowe," he spoke each name distinctly, "used three tethers. They kept the basket steady so the pilot could draw a sketch of the enemy positions. But Lowe's rival on the other side, Captain John Randolph Bryan, suffered a real shortage of equipment. So Bryan used only one tether." Chuckling, he added, "I guess that makes me a balloonist in the Dixie tradition. I like my basket to turn in the breeze. Makes it more interesting for the passengers!"

Higley went on about ballooning, explaining the various components of his rig: the valve rope to open the valve at the top of the balloon; the red rip panel rope to collapse the balloon on landing and thus prevent it from bouncing on the ground or taking off again; and the instrument box hanging outside of the basket which contained, among other items, the megaphone, a compass, and the knife used to cut loose the sand bags. Higley's commentary helped take Joshua's mind off his queasiness.

Feeling more at ease with his circumstances, he asked, "How high do you plan to take us tonight? A couple hundred feet?"

"That'd be a mere start," Higley replied. "I've got enough rope down there to go a full nine hundred feet off the ground."

Joshua flinched.

Higley continued. "Of course, we can stop at two hundred, if you'd rather. That'd be about . . . a hundred feet higher than we are right now."

Deborah shook her head in protest. "We'd be barely above the trees! *Promise* you'll take us all the way up!"

"That's up to your friends," Higley replied, his gaze seeking out Joshua.

Unwilling to be a spoilsport, Joshua said, "I suppose nine hundred feet wouldn't be so bad."

Caroline squeezed his hand, sensing a depth of reluctance his words tried to hide. She searched for something of interest to distract him, pointing to the cornfield behind her father's house. "Joshua, look! A doe and two fawns!"

He chuckled nervously. "Somebody ought to warn them about grazing on green corn."

Studying the landscape with obvious interest, Taman said, "There seem to be plenty of lakes round about. What's the name of that one?" He indicated a long, narrow body of water just south of town, his gaze coming to rest on Joshua.

"That's Duncan Lake," Joshua replied, growing somewhat accustomed to the ever-increasing altitude. Releasing his hand from Caroline's, he pointed to a tiny lake in the village. "That one's Emmons, and that lake with the tail to the north is Campau."

"Emmons and Campau," Taman repeated idly.

Caroline spoke up. "Campau Lake is where the Pioneer Association picnic is always held."

Joshua explained further. "Every August, thousands of people from Kent and Barry Counties come to hear the old settlers tell their tales." More at ease now, and no longer in competition with the band which was taking a break, Joshua continued to comment on the unfolding view—the railroad tracks winding down to Middleville and up to Grand Rapids; Cherry Valley and Kraft Avenues traversing the rural countryside north and south; 84th and 100th Streets cutting across prime farmlands in an east-west direction; and the Thornapple River flowing through scenic, hilly areas east of the village. He'd begun pointing out the various farms—George Geib's, Samuel Johnson's, Charles Kinsey's, and Jacob Vollwiler's—when a panicky shout rose clearly from the ground below.

"Zimri! Watch out!"

Joshua looked down. Straight below, his brother, caught by the ankle in a coil of tether, was being dragged toward the windlass. Joshua's heart stopped.

Panic set in below.

Higley raised his megaphone.

"Cut the tether!"

A member of his ground crew pulled out a pocket knife and hacked futilely at the thick, hemp rope.

Heart pounding now, Joshua watched helplessly as his brother slipped closer and closer to the windlass.

CHAPTER

6

Flipping open the lid of the instrument box, Higley pulled out his knife and quickly cut the tether.

With a jerk, the balloon floated free.

Joshua's stomach seemed to plummet.

On the ground, he could see his brother—only inches from the windlass—disentangle himself and limp away.

Caroline released an anxious breath. "Thank the Lord, he's not seriously hurt."

Joshua nodded, his stomach quieting. It was then that he realized his right hand was buried deep in his pocket, clenching the tattered ace of diamonds. His lucky charm had spared him misfortune again.

But a new problem had emerged—that of the untethered balloon which rose higher and higher by the minute. His gaze met Higley's. "How are we gonna get down?"

Higley smiled. "Cool air will bring us down. Might as well be patient and enjoy the ride. Looks like you folks are the only ones who are going to get a trip in my balloon this evening."

Joshua rubbed the ace of diamonds between his fingers, hoping an extra measure of luck would put him and the others safely on the ground again.

Caroline silently prayed for God's mercy to set them down without mishap.

Taman spoke up. "Higley, when was the last time you landed a free-floating balloon?"

Higley shrugged. "Don't rightly remember. I've been doing captive balloon rides for quite a spell." After a moment's thought, he added, "But don't you worry. For years, I flew free-floating balloons filled with gas while my misses performed on a trapeze. We generally got down without a fuss." He jiggled the valve line, then the rip-panel line, evidently checking for tangles.

As the balloon rose beyond the limits of earthly sounds, Caroline noticed the peacefulness, a stillness she could have enjoyed, were it not for her underlying apprehension.

Higley, evidently eager to ease the strain of a tense silence, began to talk again. "At least we don't have it as bad as Captain Bryan on *his* free flight. He blew hither and yon between the Yankees and the Confederates. Then he thought he had it made when he started to land near a Dixie encampment." Higley explained how the Confederates mistook Bryan for a Union spy and began firing on him. He eventually reached safety, landing in an orchard near Williamsburg, Virginia, where he borrowed a horse to report his findings.

Higley continued. "Lowe, the Union balloonist, figured he'd avoid Bryan's problem by putting red and white stripes and white stars on his basket."

Deborah spoke up. "So that's how you got the idea for the stars and stripes on your basket! But why did you choose yellow and purple?"

Higley smiled. "They remind me of Easter, the risen Lord. I know my balloon is just a manmade effort to rise to the heavens, but I feel closer to my Savior when I'm up here."

Taman's mouth curved in a wry smile. "Just so long as we don't get *too* close. I'd hate to think we're about to meet Him face to face."

"Not tonight," Higley said confidently. Pulling a pair of field glasses out of his instrument box, he studied a moving speck on the ground. "My crew is chasing us with the wagon. At least we won't have to scare up a ride back to the village when this is over." He passed the glasses to Joshua, then continued his stories of famous balloonists.

While Higley told of John Wise, a Lancaster, Pennsylvania man who developed the rip panel after a tangled valve line had broken off above his reach, Caroline's thoughts drifted to Higley's profession of Christ. She took solace knowing he was a believer. But she couldn't be sure about Taman. Silently, she thanked God for Higley's faith, and prayed that Taman, too, was a follower of Jesus. Her focus returned to Higley as he told about a ballooning couple by the name of Myers.

"Carl and Carlotta have a balloon farm in Indiana where they manufacture balloons—the best in the country. They made this one," he said proudly. "Carl's claim to fame was building rain-making balloons back in '91 and '92. Then, last year he was manager of the Aeronautical Concourse at the Louisiana Purchase Exposition in St. Louis."

Taman spoke up. "Didn't his wife operate the captive

balloon there?"

"That's right!" Higley exclaimed. "You were at the Exposition, then?"

Taman nodded. "The whole season. I went up in Carlotta's balloon more than once. We had a great view of the fairgrounds—Festival Hall, the Palace of Art—a much better view than from the Observation Wheel."

Higley asked, "What business were you in that kept you at the fair for the season?"

"I was in the—"

Deborah cut him off. "--Theater business, right? Musical shows, plays, vaudeville, and the like."

Taman hesitated for the slightest instant before nodding. "That's right, theater. My uncle and I ran a small theater adjacent to the grounds." He leaned over the basket, focusing on the scene below through Higley's field glasses. "We must be losing altitude. That river—what did you call it, Joshua? The Apple-something?"

"Thornapple."

"The Thornapple. It looks wider than before."

Higley pointed to an empty pasture east of the river bound by water on one side, and a road on the other. "I'll try to set us down in that field. Farmer's get mighty touchy when you upset their milk cows or damage their crops." Indicating the barn and farmhouse north of the pasture, he added, "And we sure don't want to wind up on some rooftop!" He pulled the valve rope, allowing the balloon to descend more rapidly in order to make his target.

Joshua tried to forget about his stomach, which seemed to remain aloft longer than the balloon, and borrowed the field glasses from Taman to search for the chase crew. They were creeping eastward along 84th Street just north of town. Moments later, the basket brushed the treetops on the west side of the river.

Higley swiftly hacked off three sandbags, allowing an increase in altitude. Then, a change in wind direction sent the balloon on a path that kept it above the river, preventing it from reaching the other side. To make matters worse, the riverbanks had suddenly grown steep. Twice more Higley lopped off sandbags, until the last of the ballast hit the water with a splash.

"Soon as we drift near the shore, I'm jumping out," he warned.

Joshua's heart raced. "But how do we land—"

"When you clear the bank, pull the red rope!" Higley instructed, climbing onto the edge of the basket. It dipped a trifle, skimming the surface, then an updraft provided a few feet of altitude. Moments later, a change in wind direction carried them toward the eastern bank. Higley leaped, landing with a splash in knee-deep water.

The balloon rose, scraping its way to the top of the incline where the pasture of the Loring farm lay.

Caroline prayed fervently for a soft landing.

Joshua clutched the ace of diamonds in his pocket.

The instant the basket gained the pasture, Joshua reached for the red rope, forgetting that he still held the tattered playing card. Taman grabbed for the rope, too, his hand colliding with Joshua's, knocking the ace loose from his grip.

The good luck charm flew off in the breeze.

Heart sinking, Joshua pulled down on the rip-panel rope, collapsing the balloon with Taman's help. The basket landed upright with a thud, the silk envelope fluttering to the ground like an empty sail.

The jolt would have knocked Caroline off balance, except for Joshua's strong arms catching her, steadying her on her feet. Taman did the same for Deborah, who laughed like a child on a merry-go-round.

"That was such fun, I wish we could do it all over again!" She laughed some more, and Taman smiled down at her with a too-fond look.

Caroline, despite her disapproval, fell into laughter, too, now that the danger had passed.

Joshua, infected by the lilting sound of Caroline's staccato-like levity, began to chuckle in spite of himself.

The hilarity had begun to die down when Higley climbed over the top of the bank, his trousers caked to the knee with mud, his shoes squeaking with each step. He pulled his top hat off his head, wiping perspiration from his forehead with the sleeve of his tailcoat. "Sure glad *you* folks had a happy landing."

Pointing to his filthy pants, Deborah's hysterics re-ignited, causing another round of laughter that made Caroline's sides ache. When she finally gained control of herself, she told Higley, "We didn't mean to make fun at your expense. It's just that . . . " she struggled to suppress a giggle.

He waved off her apology. Setting his hat back on his head, he opened the door to the basket, then solicited the help of Joshua and Taman in gathering up the balloon. When they had stuffed it into the basket, Joshua went off by himself as if searching the field for some lost object. Caroline joined him.

"What are you looking for, Joshua?"

"An ace of diamonds," he replied, his focus never shifting from the stubbly field.

"An ace of diamonds? But why?"

"It's my good luck charm."

"But there's no such thing as—"

Joshua's gaze met hers. "I don't expect you to understand, but would you please help me find it?"

Seeing the distressed look on his face, she began to search, too. A minute later, a sliver of white caught her eye and she bent to discover a worn-out playing card that had come to rest between two chicory weeds.

She studied the card for a moment. It was bent and smudged and had lost three of its corners. She called to Joshua.

"I've found it! I've found your ace!"

He hustled to claim it, his face a picture of relief as he rubbed the card between his fingers then tucked it in his pocket.

Caroline shook her head in puzzlement. "You're right. I don't understand. What's so special about that old playing card?"

"I told you, it's my good-luck charm," he reiterated, nudging her toward the basket where the others were waiting.

Caroline's hand on his arm, she stalled. "Joshua, I have something important to tell you."

Her sweet, yet solemn tone brought him to a halt, his gaze meeting her earnest one. "What is it?"

"There's no such thing as luck, Joshua."

He wanted to argue, but her obvious sincerity gave him pause.

She continued. "There are blessings and there are burdens. There is good, and there is evil. But to call blessings and goodness, luck—you're cheating God!"

"Cheating God?" Joshua replied, incredulous at the insult. "I do no such thing! Besides, God gave me this card!" He started toward the others.

Caroline hurried after him, struggling to find the words that would make him understand. But her thoughts were interrupted by the arrival of Higley's chase crew, his wagon turning off the road onto the field, then rattling to a halt beside the wicker basket.

Within minutes, the balloon had been loaded onto the bed at the rear of the wagon. Caroline and the others settled onto the two forward bench seats. Joshua said little on the way back to the village, leaving Caroline to ponder the unwanted pairing of Deborah and Taman, sitting too close to one another in front of her. As they rolled into the village, she could hear the band playing Sousa. Turning onto Center Street, she realized that a sizable crowd remained in front of the hotel. The moment they caught sight of the chase wagon, cheers and applause filled the air, and Professor Neron struck up a special fanfare of welcome.

Caroline's father lifted her down from the wagon, setting her on the ground with a hug. "Are you all right, Orange Blossom? You didn't get hurt when that balloon came down, did you?"

Momentarily distracted by the sight of Zimri limping over to greet Joshua, Caroline smiled up at her father. "All's well. It was really kind of exciting!"

Her mother, brother, and sister-in-law demanded hugs of their own, full of questions that were interrupted when Taman and Deborah joined them. Removing her hand from the crook of his arm, he brushed a kiss against her knuckles, then released her with a slight bow. "Good bye, Miss Dapprich. Glad to have made your acquaintance. I wish you and your cousin success with your music academy." He headed back to the hotel, threading his way through the crowd, pausing once to glance back and wave.

Caroline thought she detected moisture in her cousin's eyes as she waved in return, but her tone was unexpectedly casual. "I really enjoyed Mr. Taman's company, but it's just as well he's going back to Ohio tomorrow." Linking one arm in Caroline's, the other in her aunt's, she said, "I sure hope there's some orange layer cake left. I could use a treat after all we've been through since dinner."

Ottilia smiled. "I'm certain Vida can find you a piece, dear."

The street concert over, Joshua, Zimri, and Solon again headed to the room above Bolden & Sons Furniture and Hardware. While Zimri dealt the cards, Joshua opened windows front and back to clear the hot, stuffy air that had collected on the second floor. When he sat down and picked up the cards he'd been dealt, he could hardly believe what he discovered. There, beneath his hand, were a set of round trip Michigan Central tickets good for Detroit. His jaw hung open for a full five seconds before he spoke.

"Where did these come from?"

Zimri and Solon exchanged grins, then Zimri explained. "Solon and I figured they'd make as good a graduation present as any."

"Graduation isn't until next Friday."

"I know. We were going to wait, but the way things were going for me earlier tonight, I figured my luck might run out before then."

Joshua's gaze moved from Zimri, to Solon, and back. "I . . . thanks!" He studied them for a moment before

51

tucking them into his pocket alongside the tattered ace of diamonds, images of a brand new horseless carriage filling his mind.

At half past midnight, Neal Taman pocketed his winnings from the poker table and left the hot, smoky, Caledonia Hotel saloon. Raucous voices from the bar faded and the cool night air helped to clear his head as he strolled down Lake Street toward Railroad Street. Crossing the Michigan Central tracks, he paused to ponder the sprawling house on the hill, its shadow revealed by the light of the street lamp.

The image of Caroline Chappell's delicate and thoroughly innocent face came easily to mind along with the sound of her talented fingers moving flawlessly across the piano keyboard in her performance of Bach's *Invention Number Eight*. Such ponderings stirred a dark desire within.

Forcing the Chappell girl from mind, he recalled the comely look of her cousin, instead. The thought of Deborah Dapprich, the sound of her angelic voice, provided satisfaction of its own. Proceeding down the street past the house, he doubled back to the tennis court and garden, stooped beside the bed of pansies near the wrought iron bench, and tucked a small envelope beneath the foliage. Leaving the way he had come, he returned to his room for his bag, settled his account at the desk, then headed west on Center Street. It was the long way to the depot, he knew, but he relished a few extra minutes in the cool night air before confining himself to a passenger car for the long trip ahead. He was about to turn onto Railroad Street when he heard voices behind him. The familiar sound of Joshua

Bolden's rang out in greeting.

"Good evening, Mr. Taman!"

"Mr. Bolden," he tipped his hat, noticing that the boy's brother and a friend were with him.

"Taking the 1:15 East?" Joshua wanted to know.

Taman nodded. "And what brings you out at such a late hour? Traveling plans, as well?"

The young man shook his head. "Going home." He indicated the two-story house with Queen Ann bric-a-brac at the end of the business district.

"Been a pleasure knowing you." Giving a casual wave, he stepped off the curb, jealousy rearing over the obvious regard Caroline Chappell held for the lad.

Again, shoving thoughts of her from mind, he continued on his way, wondering what new opportunities awaited him at the next stop on his itinerary.

CHAPTER

7

Walking home from school on the day before graduation, Caroline and her cousin had just passed Dr. Breckon's house and turned the corner at the end of Johnson Street when Deborah halted abruptly, pointing down Railroad Street.

"Caroline, look!"

Home was clearly in sight, its sweeping front porch now draped with burnt orange and walnut brown bunting that was now draped between the pillars. Caroline hurried on, pausing at the front walk to study the effect the class colors would have on her guests when they arrived later for dinner. A banner hung prominently beneath the bunting, its bold, brown lettering precisely as she had requested. She read it out loud.

"Congratulations, Class of 'Naughty Five!'"

"I can hardly believe tomorrow night is our commencement!" Deborah remarked.

"I'm ready," Caroline declared. "Just think. We've already got ten students signed up for music lessons here at the house, and another five who want us to come to their homes. And we're bound to find more, once we've gotten started."

Ignoring the topic, Deborah hurried up the walk, dragging Caroline with her. "Let's see how things look inside.

Your mother promised the house would be rich in class colors by the time we got home."

Caroline followed her cousin through the front door, discovering that her mother had indeed kept her promise. The vestibule and staircase were dressed up with orange and brown crepe paper swags, as was the front parlor. In addition, a photograph collection of class members from grammar school days had been artfully arranged on the center table.

"Look!" Deborah exclaimed, pointing to the silk butterflies that adorned the corners of each framed picture. "These will certainly give us plenty to talk about when our guests arrive."

"That, they will," Caroline agreed, pleased at the method her mother had found to ease the first awkward moments of the evening.

Class colors and decorative butterflies dominated the dining room, also. Crepe paper swags connected the chandelier to various points along the plaster cornice above the Anaglypta frieze, giving the impression of a false paper ceiling. The silk shade on the light above the table—normally pale green--had been replaced with one of pale orange trimmed with silk Monarchs. And on the table, which was long enough to seat all sixteen members of the graduating class, four centerpieces of day lilies and four pair of orange tapered candles set off the damask tablecloth which had also been dyed a pale orange.

Each place setting featured a single day lily in a vial of water tied up with a brown satin bow, and a leather bookmark—the class souvenir. They were stamped with "Class of '05," the letters and numbers illuminated in burnt orange enamel. In the center of every place setting, propped against the peach-colored napkins that had been folded to stand erect, was a four-course menu neatly lettered in calligraphy on pale peach card stock and embossed with a butterfly in the corner.

Caroline read the menu out loud. "Oysters and clear soup. Poached salmon and boiled potatoes. Chicken croquettes with asparagus. Apricots with whipped cream. Orange ice cream. Chocolate cake."

At the sound of her voice, her mother emerged from the library, pale orange place cards, a vial of brown ink, and two pens in hand. "You girls are just in time to do the lettering of your classmates' names."

Deborah slipped past her. "Caroline will do it, Aunt Ottilia. You know how awful I am at calligraphy. I'll see if Vida can use my help in the kitchen."

Caroline reached for the cards. "The dining room looks marvelous, Mother! Did you by any chance have time to decorate the music room the way we discussed?"

Ottilia smiled. Leading Caroline to the closed pocket door, she slid it back with a dramatic gesture. "Voilà!"

Caroline gasped. The effect was stunning. Orange and brown velvet draped the grand piano, setting off white marble busts of Bach, Mozart, and Beethoven, each of whom was sporting an orange and brown bow-tie. Beside the great masters were presents wrapped in orange tissue and brown ribbon for the winners of the games her guests would play. Her music rack had been decorated, too, in orange and brown crepe paper, more of which was hanging in fringe-like streamers from the arms of the electrolier. The most dramatic decoration of all, however, was the six-foot long brass bugle resting in a bracket against the moulded panel wall. From it hung a long, brown velvet banner appliqued in burnt orange with "Class of 1905." Beneath the lettering, the banner came to a point, and there hung a thick, orange and brown satin tassel—a fat version of the ones that would hang from the graduates' mortarboards on commencement day.

Caroline set down the place cards and hugged her mother. "It's perfect! Thank you!"

"You're welcome, dear! You only graduate from high school once. You might as well have your party the way you want it!"

Gathering place cards, pen, and ink together, Caroline headed for the stairs. "I'll be back with these shortly. Then I'm going to bathe and dress. Is my—"

"Your dress is pressed, and so is Deborah's. Now off with you! And don't forget—your guests will be here at a quarter till six. That's less than an hour and a half away."

"I'll be ready!" she promised, hurrying up the stairs.

Time evaporated more quickly than Caroline anticipated. She was helping Deborah decide on the best place to fasten her butterfly pin when the front doorbell chimed.

Her cousin pointed to the clock on her dresser. "Look! It's only twenty-five minutes past five! Who do you suppose had the audacity to show up so unfashionably early?"

"I don't know, but we must go down and welcome them. And don't you dare speak a single word about how early it is!" Caroline cautioned.

A minute later, they opened the door to find a young girl, hair covered by a scarf, apron soiled as if she'd spent the day cooking and cleaning. Focus fixed on Caroline, she said, "I dunno if you remember me. I'm Tess Johnson. I was at your recital."

"Miss Johnson! Of course! Won't you come in?"

She shook her head. "May I speak with you alone a minute?"

Deborah excused herself and Caroline stepped out onto the porch. "What can I do for you, Miss Johnson? Have you come to sign up for piano lessons?"

Tess shifted her weight. "If you'll have me. But I ain't got no money to pay for them. My employer, Mrs. Graybiel, she said I ought to come see you, and ask you if there's some way I could earn my lessons by helping clean house, or some such."

Before Caroline could reply, Tess rushed on. "I'm a real good worker. Mrs. Graybiel, she'll vouch for that. She says I can use her pie-anna for practicing. I ain't got no pie-anna of my own, but if I could just take a few lessons, I'm sure I could catch on real quick, and . . . What do you think? Can you teach me? 'Course, I don't read too good, but I figure I don't really need to know words to play the pie-anna. All I got to do is learn how to read notes. Ain't that right, Miss Chappell?"

"I . . . uh . . . " Caroline struggled to take in all that Tess had said, praying for the right response. Inspiration dawning, she asked, "Are you willing to practice an hour a day, each and every day?"

Tess nodded vigorously.

"And can you be here at 8 AM sharp, each and every Monday morning?"

"Oh, yes, Miss Chappell, I can be here!"

"Then I'll see you next Monday morning at eight!"

"Thank you, Miss Chappell! Thank you so much!" She hurried away so quickly, she nearly stumbled down the porch steps. Catching her balance just in time to avoid a fall, she turned to wave good-bye, then hurried toward Johnson Street.

Caroline went inside to tell Deborah and her mother about her newest student. She was halfway through her description when the doorbell chimed again. This time, she and Deborah opened the door to find Joshua and Solon.

Joshua was expecting Caroline to look especially nice, but the sight of her caught him dumbfounded. Her dress, predominantly a sort of peach-colored lace, really set off her dark hair and eyes. She was so pretty, his hands began to shake. He nearly dropped the chipboard box he was holding. But he scrambled to catch it before it hit the porch, a sheepish smile overtaking him.

Caroline was completely taken aback by Joshua's stately good looks. His grey flannel suit, evidently brand new and tailored to perfection, added dignity to his youthful charm. This more mature look was so out-of-keeping with the clumsy slip of his hands that she had to work extra hard to suppress a nervous giggle over the faux pas.

Deborah, evidently sensitive to her cousin's plight, turned attention on herself by linking her arm in Solon's. "Let me show you the photograph collection in the parlor. I think you'll find it very interesting."

With the others gone, Joshua offered his gift to Caroline, his voice trembling when he spoke. "I . . . I hope these will be all right."

He nearly shoved the small carton into her hands. She accepted it with a smile, desperate to put him at ease. Carefully lifting the lid, she found a corsage of tiny roses in the same delicate shade of peach as her dress. They were tied with several loops of brown and peach satin ribbon against layers of matching netting. Carefully, she lifted the flowers from their nest of shredded tissue and turned to the hall tree mirror to pin them in place.

Her own hands were unsteady as she threaded the corsage pins through stems and fabric, but she managed to accomplish the task without a pin prick, turning to face Joshua again. "This corsage is the loveliest I've ever seen. I'll keep it always, as a remembrance of a very special evening."

Her words, delivered in a soft, throaty whisper, stirred Joshua in a way he'd never known. He reached for her hand, enveloping it firmly in both of his.

His touch sent a surge of warmth through Caroline, drawing her to him with a force she couldn't resist. Mere inches separated her mouth from his, and she was certain his lips were about to meet hers when the doorbell chimed.

Reluctantly, Joshua released Caroline, turmoil raging within over the kiss gone unfulfilled, and the guilt he'd have carried if he'd succeeded in taking advantage of a young lady to whom he was not promised.

With a prayer of thanks for divine intervention, Caroline answered the door. In a steady stream, the other twelve classmates—many of whom she'd known since the age of eight—made their entrance: Roy and Gordon, Anna and Mary, Pearl and Sada, Frank and Blaine, Edna and Louretta, Edward and Arthur. And though she greeted them with a sunny smile and cheerful words of welcome, she was privately disappointed with herself for being so vulnerable to Joshua's advances. Determined to save her first kiss until after betrothal, she knew she must avoid potentially compromising circumstances in the future.

Joshua sensed a slight change in Caroline. She sat next to him at dinner, then spent most of her time talking to

Deborah and Solon. At least his friend was enjoying himself. And Deborah seemed to like his attention.

But Joshua was uneasy. He held back when Caroline led her guests to the music room for entertainment. He waited for everyone else to take a seat before claiming the last one by the door. Seeing Joshua's tentative restraint, Caroline offered him a smile, then sounded a chord on the piano to gain her guests' attention. When all was quiet, she told them brightly, "We're about to play a game of music identification!"

She passed out paper and pencils while Deborah rolled a tea cart to the center of the room. On it were several miscellaneous objects, each identified with a number.

Caroline explained. "Each item represents a term in music." She held up a ruler as an example. "You have fifteen minutes to write down your answers."

While guests congregated around the table making quips about the puzzling collection of items displayed, Solon was never far from Deborah. Caroline hoped his interest in her cousin would continue beyond this evening, believing Solon could be a leveling influence on Deborah's more flighty ways.

When the quarter hour had passed and Caroline collected the answer sheets, she realized her game had stumped her classmates more thoroughly than anticipated. Nevertheless, one of the pages was completely filled in. Though it had no name, she recognized Joshua's handwriting.

"We have a winner," she announced, "but before I award the prize, let's identify the musical meaning for each of the objects. Everyone knows what this is," she stated, holding up a picture of a baseball player about to throw a ball.

"Pitch!" came a chorus of replies.

One by one, she revealed the answers to the puzzle. Ruler—measure. Fish skin—scales. A ball of twine—cord (chord). A heavy walking stick--staff. A butcher's knife--sharp. The base of a column cut from a picture—bass. Several squares of soap—bars. A picture of Rip Van Winkle asleep—rest.

Holding up Joshua's answer sheet, Caroline said, "Our class president has a perfect paper." She chose one of the wrapped gifts on the piano—a small, slender box—and presented it to him. "Congratulations!"

He nodded his thanks, stashing the parcel in his pocket until his classmates demanded that he open it.

Cheeks flush, he complied, revealing a silver fountain pen with two lines of engraving:

Caledonia High School
Class of 1905

"I . . . thanks!" was all he managed to say before his classmates insisted on passing it around for everyone to see.

When all had had their chance, Deborah handed out more paper while Caroline explained the next game.

"You have five minutes to write down as many words as you can, formed from the letters in the word, Symphony."

This time, Solon won, his prize a note clip made from thick brass wire bent into the shape of a G clef.

While he passed it amongst his classmates, Caroline excused herself, returning moments later bearing a large silver tray upon which were arranged several brown, leather-bound booklets, each bearing a name painted in burnt orange enamel of a class member. Attached to the spine of each book was a loop holding a fountain pen.

"And now, for the last activity of the evening," she announced. "Before we part, I thought it would be a nice idea to get each others' autographs. And for that purpose, I would like each of you to have a new autograph book."

Her classmates accepted her gifts with heartfelt thanks, each set immediately to the task of getting the autographs of all the other members of the class. An hour later, Caroline had exchanged autographs with every classmate but two--Deborah and Joshua. Assuming she would get Deborah's after the party ended, she sought out Joshua, finding him in the chair nearest the door where he'd begun the evening. There, he sat poring over the inscriptions freshly written on the pages of his book.

She sat beside him, her book extended. "I'd be most honored if you'd grace one of the pages of my book with your inscription."

He nodded, exchanging his own book for hers. Taking in hand the new silver pen he'd won as his prize, he turned to the back of her book and paused. Caroline was already writing furiously in his own book.

He wished he were a poet. Maybe then, he'd know the fancy words to describe his feelings. But he was no poet. The words that came to him were plain and simple. Slowly, he began to put them down. He was not yet finished when Caroline closed his own book.

She wasn't ready for Joshua to see what she had written to him just yet. But her guests were ready to leave, and she needed to see them out the door. Instead of returning his autograph book to him, she said, "Would you please stay after the party? I'd like to return your book after our classmates have gone."

He nodded, pausing to say good night to his friends, then following Deborah and Solon outside to the peace and quiet of the garden. While they strolled the rose-bordered paths, quietly talking and laughing, he took a seat on the white iron bench and put the finishing words to the sentiments he was composing. He had just put away his pen when Caroline came to sit beside him. Her brown eyes, so often sparkling with excitement, were thoughtful as they exchanged books.

Caroline flipped through the pages, finally finding Joshua's entry inside the back cover. He'd composed an acrostic of her name which she read with great interest.

Caroline makes beautiful music, and
Always stays in
Rhythm.
Orange is her favorite color. She's
Lovely as the day is long.
I
Never will forget the girl who is
Ever ready to play a song. From J.B.

Joshua wasn't a bit surprised to find a G clef marking the corner of the page where Caroline had signed his book. Her entry read like a letter, and he weighed each of her words carefully.

Dear Joshua,
A curious thing happened when we were about to play together in my recital. I suddenly realized

that I was going to miss making music with you.
I will have students to teach. I will play the organ in
church when Mrs. Barber can't be there. I might
even compose a new sonata. But it won't be the same
as when we were practicing for my recital.

Now that we are about to graduate from high school,
I have discovered something else. I am going to
miss seeing you every day. I know that you will
be only a short distance away, working in your father's
store, but it won't be like it was, seeing you in class.

I wish you God's blessings in your future endeavors,
and I pray you will not mistake His grace for luck
invoked by that ace of diamonds you carry in
your pocket.   Fondly, Caroline.

Joshua's heart played a bar of sixteenth notes. Caroline
was fond of him. He'd suspected it. Now he knew for
certain.

A vision of great-grandpa's chest came to mind, all
stained in burnt orange. He'd been biding his time, waiting
for her recital to be over and graduation to pass to begin a
proper courtship. Maybe the time was now.

When he finally looked up, Caroline's uncertain gaze
was on him, watching for his reaction. He reached for her
hand. Encouraged by the firm manner in which she
grasped his own, he began to speak.

"Caroline, I . . . I'm not much with words," he began,
wishing he had his trumpet. Then he'd put his feelings into
music. The notes would soar to high C, maybe higher. But
this was no time for music. He needed words. The *right*
words. He prayed they'd come, then he continued. "What
you said about not seeing each other every day, and not

making music . . . it doesn't have to be like that if we don't want it to." He drew a tight breath. "What I'm trying to say, is . . . I'd like to call on you, if that'd be all right." Caroline's smile reached all the way to her eyes, glistening now with moisture born of happiness. "Yes! You may call on me!" Her smile lasted a few seconds longer, turning suddenly dark. Freeing her hand from his, she shook her finger at him. "There is one thing that bothers me."

His brows came together.

"You needn't look so worried," she scolded, laughing her staccato laugh. Then she grew solemn once more. "Tonight, before the party began, there was a moment in the front hall when I thought you might . . . "

Joshua lowered his gaze. Feeling morally obligated to admit the truth, he quietly told her, "I wanted to kiss you."

She replied in a half-whisper. "And I wanted you to, but I *didn't* want you to. Am I making any sense?"

"Perfect sense."

She sighed sweetly, lifting his chin to capture his gaze. "Promise me you won't kiss me, Joshua."

"Never?"

"Not never. Just not until I'm ready."

"I promise."

With that, she pecked him on the cheek, then flitted away, dancing down the garden path toward Deborah and Solon, a happy tune on her lips.

In her room later that evening, she was still elated over Joshua's request to come calling when Deborah came up to undress for bed.

"You must like Solon," Caroline commented, setting hairbrush aside and flipping back the orange summer coverlet on her bed.

"He's very nice," Deborah admitted. Autograph book in hand, she approached her cousin. "You're the only classmate who hasn't signed my book."

"Nor have you signed mine. It's in the top drawer of my dresser," she explained, sliding Deborah's pen from its sleeve. Page by page, she read each of the autographs written to her cousin. Most of them referred to the short but pleasant time she had spent in the Class of '05, or her excellent singing voice. Solon mentioned both.

Sorry the Class of '05 couldn't have benefited
longer from your singing talent. I'm sure it will
take you far! Solon.

Joshua's sentiments were along the same lines. Caroline paused to consider the words she wanted to share with her cousin, then applied pen to paper, artfully forming the letters in calligraphy style.

Dearest Cousin Deborah,
Together, we shall raise the standards for music in
Caledonia, making this a truly cultural community!
Love and affection, Caroline.

Seeing that Deborah was still reading the autographs in her own book but had not yet signed it, she lay her cousin's book on her dresser and climbed into bed.

Seconds later, Deborah turned out the light, saying, "I'm going to wait until tomorrow to sign your book. Good night."

"Good night, cousin. Sweet dreams, of Solon, that is!"

"Oh, hush!" came Deborah's response.

Twenty-four hours later, as Caroline prepared for bed after the graduation ceremony and reception at the Methodist Episcopal Church, she still couldn't believe that she was finished with high school forever. That morning, she had played the piano for the last time for a school assembly. And only three short hours ago, she and Deborah had marched down the aisle of the church in pale orange graduation caps and gowns. Tucking hers away in the back of her closet, she recalled visions of the fellows in their class, all dressed in their coffee-colored gowns. A handsomer crew she'd never seen, especially Joshua, who appeared almost professorial when giving his Class President's speech.

Donning her nightgown, she reached for the book Parker and Roxana had given her as a graduation gift. It was good to have them home again for the weekend. Caroline enjoyed the sound of Roxana's gentle laughter as she and Parker headed for their room at the end of the hall. And she loved the new book they had chosen for her, *The Encyclopedia of Music and Composers*. Plumping her pillows into a comfortable backrest against the head board, she sat down on her bed to browse, starting with Johann Sebastian Bach.

She had arrived at the chapter on Beethoven when Deborah entered the bedroom, full of conversation. "When I came here two months ago, I sure didn't think I'd be graduating at the end of this school year. I have you to thank for this." She held up her diploma, still tied in a scroll with a length of orange satin ribbon.

Caroline closed her book and set it on the bed stand.

"And now that we're finished with school, we can get started with our music academy! Aren't you excited about your new students? Rhea Kinsey will be a delight, and so will Celesta Oldt."

"I'm not so sure about some of *your* students, though," Deborah responded, "with that Tess Johnson showing up first thing Monday morning." She set her diploma on the dresser, then removed the tassel from her mortarboard and placed it alongside. With a wide yawn, she reached for Caroline's autograph book which lay on her vanity.

"Maybe you'd better just get undressed and crawl into bed," Caroline suggested. "Your autograph can wait until tomorrow."

Deborah shook her head. "I know what I want to say, and I'm going to write it down before I forget. But I'll do it in the library so as not to disturb you. Good night." She paused by the door, her gaze lingering on Caroline before she clicked off the light and left the room.

When Caroline awoke the following morning, she thought it odd that Deborah's bed was empty. In the two months since she'd come to Caledonia, she'd never been the first one up in the morning. Thinking her cousin had gone to the bathroom, Caroline rose and headed for her closet, noticing in the process that her autograph book lay on her dresser, the pen tucked between the pages. Caroline opened it to the marked place. Deborah's handwriting filled the page accented with butterfly sketches.

Dearest Cousin Caroline,
    I couldn't have asked for a nicer, more talented cousin. No wonder Joshua wants to court you! The

two of you were meant for each other.

Thank you for all the help you've given me, getting me through my studies and including me in your recital. I didn't deserve all the love and kindness you shared.

I know you will be successful with the music academy. I'm honored that you invited me to be a part of it, but I cannot.

I've gone to seek my future elsewhere. I must do what will make me happy. Please don't be angry with me for following my own dream.

Love always, your cousin, Deborah.

Panic setting in, Caroline checked the closet. Two of Deborah's hangers were empty, and her favorite butterfly embroidery, the one which had occupied the center of her dresser, was gone. Tossing on a robe, Caroline hurried down the hall to check the bathroom. It was unoccupied. She raced down the steps to the first floor, going from parlor to dining room, calling Deborah's name, but to no avail.

Vida peeked out the kitchen door, the aroma of coffee and fresh-baked strudel wafting into the dining room. "Vat is wrong, *Frauline Caroline?*"

"Vida, have you seen Deborah this morning?"

The cook shook her head.

Ottilia's voice sounded from the upstairs hall. "Caroline, is something wrong?"

She called up to her mother from the foyer. "Deborah's run away!"

CHAPTER

8

"Deborah's run away?" Ottilia asked, unbelieving. "Are you sure?"

Caroline started up the stairs. "Quite sure, Mother. She even left me a good-bye note. I'll show you."

Following Caroline to her room, Ottilia read the autograph, snapped the book shut, then charged down the hall toward the master bedroom.

"Charles! Charles, get up! Deborah's run away!"

Caroline's father emerged, yawning as he pulled on a silk robe that barely covered his ample belly. "What's this about Deborah, dear?"

"She's gone! And after all we've done for her!"

"But . . . ?"

Ottilia opened to Deborah's autograph, thrusting the book into her husband's hands. "It's all right here." Too agitated to wait until he'd finished reading, she went on. "We've got to go after her! Before she's ruined her reputation!"

Still in his pajamas, Parker came down the hall, dark hair tousled, eyes sleepy. "What's all the fuss, Mother?"

"Deborah's run away. Did you hear anything last night? Anyone stirring?"

Parker shook his head.

"We've got to do something! Go after her!"

Charles put his arm about Ottilia's shoulders. "Calm down, dear. We'll find her, but not until I've had my coffee." Gaze shifting to Caroline, he asked, "Did Deborah give you any idea where she was going?"

Her mother answered for her. "To that Taman fellow in Cleveland, that's where. He put stars in her eyes with his promises of a career on the stage. I've half a mind to get on the next train headed east and drag her right back here where she belongs."

Charles shook his head. "Not so fast, dear. First, we have to make certain that she's not still right here in town."

Caroline said, "We can ask along Center Street if anyone's seen her since last night."

Parker nodded. "Good idea, Sis. I'll help just as soon as I'm dressed." He headed back down the hall.

Slipping free of her husband's embrace, Ottilia said, "Just as soon as I've made myself decent, I'm going to the depot and ask if the agent's seen her."

Charles followed his wife into the master bedroom, saying, "Suit yourself, dear, but I'm going down for some coffee. I'm no good until I've had my first cup of Vida's brew."

Caroline returned to her room to dress, still puzzled over her cousin's behavior. Reflecting on the night of their recital, she realized what an accomplished actress Deborah had already become, leading everyone to believe she had given up the idea of a life on the stage. As Caroline laid out a dark skirt and white blouse with orange tatting on the collar, she wondered when Deborah had conceived the plan to leave town. She still had come to no conclusions when her thoughts were interrupted by the sound of someone moaning with pain, and Parker's voice echoing down the hall.

"Mother! Come quick! Roxana needs you!"

Still in her petticoat and chemise, Caroline popped her head out the door. "Parker, what is it? What's wrong?"

Parker's cheeks were flush, his expression one of pure panic. "Get Mother! Roxana's bleeding . . . badly!"

Pulling on her wrapper, Caroline did as Parker asked, following her mother into Parker and Roxana's room where her sister-in-law lay restless with pain.

Ottilia was immediately at her daughter-in-law's side, stroking her forehead. "What's the matter, dear? Are you having a difficult monthly?"

Roxana shook her head, tears running down her cheeks as she clutched the bed covers to her. "I . . . I was in the family way . . . but now . . . "

Ottilia addressed Caroline. "Ring up Dr. Breckon! Tell him to come immediately. Roxana's miscarried!"

Caroline rushed to obey, pulling on blouse and skirt as hastily as possible, her legs carrying her to the telephone downstairs. In a matter of minutes, the doctor was at the door. With quick steps, he followed her upstairs to the room containing his patient. All but Ottilia were temporarily banned from Roxana's presence.

Parker, still in his robe, paced the hall. "I didn't even know Roxana was with child, and now . . . she's completely heartbroken. The worst part is, there's nothing I can do for her."

Caroline put her arm about her brother's waist. "I'm

73

sorry, Parker. I can't imagine how badly you must feel." Pausing to face him, she said, "But there *is* something you can do for Roxana."

Parker looked doubtful.

Caroline smiled briefly. "You can help her to start again on your family."

Parker pondered the suggestion before making a response. "We'll have to see what the doctor says."

Some time later, after Dr. Breckon had allowed Parker in to see his wife, Caroline went downstairs. Too hungry to search for Deborah, she helped herself to the hot tea and fresh apple strudel Vida had set out on the sideboard, then sat kitty-corner from her papa, who inquired immediately about his daughter-in-law.

"I haven't been in to see her," Caroline replied, "but Parker's with her now, so she must be improving."

Confirmation arrived moments later when Ottilia came down to see the doctor out and to fetch some tea for Parker and Roxana. "According to Dr. Breckon, Roxana will be fine after a couple of days' bed rest."

Charles nodded understandingly. "Ottilia, dear, about Deborah. I think—"

"Deborah!" she said disparagingly. "I should have known that girl would pick the most inopportune time to cause trouble. I hope you and Caroline can look for her without my help, because I'll be busy taking care of Roxana."

"Of course, dear," Charles replied, adding, "I assume you're canceling plans to attend the Summer Reception tonight."

Ottilia sighed in disappointment. "With everything else that's come up this morning, I'd completely forgotten.

Yes, I'll have to cancel--Roxana needs me." Her gaze shifting to Caroline, she said, "Why don't you go to the reception with your father? No point in letting the tickets go to waste." Not waiting for a response, she hurried upstairs.

When Ottilia had gone, Caroline's father told her, "You needn't go to the reception, unless you want to."

"I . . . " Caroline hardly knew what to say, aware that the event would be attended mostly by folks old enough to be her parents.

Her father grinned mischievously, "I just came up with an excellent idea. I'm going to ask your musician friend, the young Mr. Bolden to take you to the reception." Before Caroline could protest, he continued. "Now, about your cousin, Deborah. Let's start at the depot."

A few minutes later, arm linked with her papa's, Caroline accompanied him in the bright June sunshine to the small passenger waiting room of the Michigan Central Depot where Joseph Carey, the lanky agent, greeted them brightly. "Mr. Chappell, Miss Caroline, what can I do for you this fine day?"

Charles spoke first. "You know my niece, Deborah Dapprich, don't you? Caroline's age, but a little taller, with blond hair?"

The agent nodded. "Sure do. Heard her sing at the recital. Fine voice that girl's got—a real God-given gift."

Caroline agreed, asking, "Have you seen her get on a train this morning? She's gone off, and we thought maybe . . . "

The agent shook his head. "Been here since five, and I know for a fact she didn't get on the 5:40 goin' East, or the 5:50 goin' West."

Charles asked, "What about the other trains, the ones that come through in the middle of the night?"

Carey scratched his bony chin. "There's one at 1:15 going East. You'd have to check with my assistant, Billy White, about that one. He takes the night shift."

"Thank you very much, Mr. Carey. I'll do that."

Escorting Caroline over to Center Street, he said, "I'm going up the hill to the White place to check with Billy. Meanwhile, why don't you go across the street," he indicated Bolden & Sons Furniture and Hardware. "Ask Joshua if he or his friend, Solon, heard Deborah say anything about plans to leave town. I'll join you there, shortly."

Finding Joshua busy waiting on Emanuel Berry, the village carpenter, Caroline browsed among the furniture display. She couldn't help noticing how efficient and congenial Joshua was, weighing up several different types and sizes of nuts and bolts, ciphering the cost in his head. But concern for Deborah soon dominated her thoughts. Idly running her hand along the etched leaf pattern on a two-drawer oak cabinet, she worried whether her cousin was safe, whether she'd had anything to eat, and where she was headed. She was deep in thought when Joshua approached.

"Do you like that piece?" he asked. "It came in last week from Chicago." Her appearance in the store, so unexpected, had almost made him lose count of Mr. Berry's purchases. And standing close enough now to catch a whiff of her orange blossom toilet water made him want to take the day off, get out in the fine weather, drive her down to the river for a picnic. But Caroline's expression, pensive and somber, and the fact that she didn't even seem to hear him, put such thoughts from mind. "Is something wrong,

Caroline? I've been standing here, talking to you, but you look miles away."

Suddenly aware of Joshua's presence, Caroline looked up with a start. "Joshua, I'm sorry. I didn't mean to ignore you. It's just that . . . " Her chin trembled, and she twisted the ring on her little finger nervously.

"What is it, Caroline?" he gently prompted.

She pressed her lips together, then blinked, barely holding back sobs and tears. Drawing a tight breath, she swallowed past the constriction in her throat, words coming in fits and starts. "It's Deborah. She's gone . . . run away. What a judy I've been! I should have seen it coming . . . should have stopped her . . . I feel so responsible . . . " She turned away, struggling desperately to keep from crying.

Joshua's heart went out to her. His arm about her shoulders, he guided her toward the back room, praying no one would enter the store. With his father and brother out making a furniture delivery, he was the only one available to wait on customers. As they entered the back room, he suddenly realized that his grandfather's chest—the one he planned to someday give Caroline as a betrothal gift—was in plain view. Swiftly, he covered it with an old muslin sheet. Inviting her to sit there, he pulled up a small stool and sat facing her.

"Now what's this about Deborah running away? Why would she leave? And where would she go?"

Caroline dabbed her eyes and blew her nose, determined to maintain control as she told of her cousin's note in the autograph book, and her mother's suspicion that Deborah had gone to take up Taman's offer of a job in his Cleveland theater. "Papa's gone to see Billy White—the assistant at the depot—to find out if she took the early morning train East. He said I should ask you if you ever heard Deborah say anything about leaving."

Joshua shook his head in disbelief. "Wish I could help. I'm as surprised as you."

"Do you think Solon knows anything?"

He shrugged. "I'll ring him up."

Caroline followed him to the phone behind the front counter, but the brief conversation produced no new information. Joshua was just hanging up when her father came through the door, his expression hopeful.

"I've spoken with young Mr. White."

Caroline hurried toward him. "Did Deborah take the 1:15 East?"

Her father nodded.

Joshua joined them. "Then Mr. White sold her a ticket. Where was she bound?"

Charles shook his head thoughtfully. "You jumped to the same conclusion I did. Fact is, she already had a ticket, so there's no way of knowing whether she went all the way to Detroit, or somewhere in between. But my guess is, she went to Detroit, where she'd been living for the last couple of years before her mama died."

"Makes sense," Joshua commented. "She'd know folks there."

Caroline linked her arm affectionately with her father's. "Buy me a ticket to Detroit, Papa. I'll find her and bring her home."

"Nonsense!" he exclaimed with a wise smile.

"Mama can't go, with Roxana sick, and you can't get away until the Sutherland case is settled. *Someone's* got to go after her!" Caroline insisted.

Joshua's heart lurched at the thought that Caroline

might actually attempt a trip to such a large city, unescorted. "What about your music academy?"

Before she could reply, her father asked, "Don't you have students coming on Monday morning?"

"Yes, but—"

Her father continued. "I'll hire Pinkertons in Detroit to find her. I'll send a wire. According to Billy White, Deborah's train won't arrive for another couple of hours."

Joshua's hand in his pocket, he rubbed the tattered ace of diamonds between his fingers, hoping the agents would have good luck locating Deborah. Beside the playing card, he felt the stiffness of his own ticket to Detroit. In a week's time, he'd be headed to the skat conference. And tonight, he'd spend his time into the wee hours sharpening his skills with Solon and Zimri.

His thoughts were interrupted when Mr. Chappell produced two tickets of another sort. "Joshua, son, how would you like to escort Caroline to the Summer Reception in Kennedy Hall tonight? I was planning to take Mrs. Chappell, but with our daughter-in-law sick . . . well . . . you know how it is. Mama insists on staying home to nurse her."

"I . . . uh . . . "

Embarrassed for Joshua, Caroline scolded her father. "You're being very unfair, springing this on him at the last minute."

Joshua's gaze met Mr. Chappell's, his words discreet. "Thanks for the offer, sir, but I already have plans for this evening."

"To take another young lady?" Caroline's father asked with innocent surprise.

Joshua's cheeks grew warm. "No, sir! To . . . uh . . . "

With the curious gaze of both Chappells on him, he had no choice but to offer a full explanation. "I'm playing skat with Solon and Zimri tonight."

Caroline's brow twitched. "Skat? I've never heard of that."

Her father explained. "That's a German card game, isn't it, son?"

"Yes, sir. It's something like—"

Caroline cut him off. "A card game? You're wasting a perfectly good evening on a card game?"

"You don't understand," Joshua argued, ready to explain further when her father spoke instead.

"The rules are very complicated, Orange Blossom. From my understanding, skat takes a lot of skill. Isn't that so, Joshua?"

He nodded. "There's even a conference planned—next week in Detroit. If I'm good enough, I'll win an automobile."

Mr. Chappell smiled. "Think of that, Caroline! Joshua driving down Center Street of Caledonia in an automobile!"

"I can't imagine!" she said with disgust. "It's just as well that you're taking me to the reception tonight, Papa, because I have no intention of spending time with anyone who puts so much stock in a game of chance." She nudged her father toward the door.

Charles shrugged, telling Joshua, "Enjoy your evening, son. Maybe you *will* win an automobile!"

When they had gone, Joshua dragged an empty keg of ten-penny nails to the back room, intending to replace it with a full one when his gaze fell on the sheet covering Great-grandpa Bolden's chest. He whipped it off, turned the keg upside down, and sat to stare at the burnt-orange finish. "A lot of good you'll do me now," he grumbled. "If I win at skat, I lose with Caroline." He remembered the rainy afternoons he and Zimri and Grandpa had spent in games of skat. Anger rising, he stood abruptly, kicking the empty keg aside. "Let her think what she wants! I'm not gonna give up skat!"

Caroline spent the afternoon in the music room composing ditties for Tess Johnson's first piano lesson, all the while wondering if she was really prepared to end her association with Joshua over his card-playing habit. The saying her mother had taught her from childhood kept running through her mind. *Idle hands are the devil's workshop, and playing cards his tools.* By the end of the day, although Caroline was satisfied with the outcome of her simple compositions, her mood was considerably subdued, and she could work up little enthusiasm for attending the Summer Reception.

Nevertheless, she bathed and donned the dress she had worn for her graduation dinner, spirits lifted by her papa's compliments and smile of approval when she came downstairs. Arm linked with his, they proceeded on foot the short distance to Kennedy Hall, located above Van Amburg's Grocery and Mr. Beeler's drug store. Throughout the meal—a roast chicken dinner cooked and served by the Caledonia Hotel—and afterward when Caroline danced with her papa to the music of the Betzner and Clemens' orchestra, she thought often that it was just as well Joshua couldn't attend. The wooden floor was horribly uneven and in need of replacement, making for a very rough time dancing. The others present were fifteen or twenty years older than she, and with the exception of her discussions with two women who wished to enroll their children for piano instruction, and a mother who was disappointed to learn that Deborah would not be giving her daughter vocal lessons, Caroline contributed little to the evening's conversation.

As church time approached the following morning, she was increasingly vexed over her dilemma with Joshua. Moment by moment her opinion vacillated between anger over his serious involvement with cards, and doubt as to whether the habit was as damaging as she had been taught. She had wanted to discuss the matter with her mother, but Ottilia had been too preoccupied with Roxana's wellbeing for Caroline to broach the subject. Caroline's father had been unavailable as well, the only interruption of his early morning solitude in the library being that of her mother to insist that he hire Pinkertons in Cleveland as well as Detroit to search for Deborah.

On the way to church, beneath cloudy skies that portended an afternoon rain, Caroline prayed that Joshua would simply admit his card-playing was a waste of time and that he was giving it up. Hopes of the desired action evaporated when both Joshua and his brother failed to appear at the service with their folks. Solon wasn't in church, either, although his parents were. Caroline immediately concluded that the fellows had played cards so late into the night that they had been unable to attend the morning service, an assumption that added weight to her negative opinion of the pastime.

Silently, she fumed, too distracted to pay heed to the sermon on piety and the qualifications for entering heaven. She did manage to listen, however, when Solon's father took the pulpit to make an unexpected but pleasant announcement.

"This Thursday night, my wife and I request the pleasure of your company at our place for a strawberry social! Come about seven, stay till the strawberries are gone. See you there!"

Solon's folks had a tradition of putting on the most delightful strawberry socials in the village, Caroline knew, and she made a mental note to go, hoping Joshua would be there, also. But the bright thought faded beneath increasingly gray clouds on the walk home, and was further pressed from mind the following morning during Tess Johnson's very first music lesson.

Promptly at eight, the young girl arrived amidst a noisy thunderstorm, and Caroline quickly learned that it would take more than thunder to drown out the girl's heavy hand on the ivories. Their hour together, ponderous at first as Caroline reminded her repeatedly to lighten her touch, eventually passed with satisfactory results. Tess managed to play through an entire piece without one note louder than *forte*. She learned the meanings of this and other musical terms as well, such as *andante, allegro,* and *largo*. By the time Tess's hour was up, Caroline was looking forward to the girl's next lesson, eager to see how well she would progress in a week, practicing on her own.

But time dragged. By Thursday, Caroline felt as though she'd been living her life at *tempo largo*. She pondered the point as she sought relief from the hot, still air in the music room. Her last student of the week having gone for the day, she exited to the veranda. The earthy scent of dark geranium from her mother's hanging pot tinged the air. Sinking down in a wicker chair, she fanned herself with her handkerchief and thought.

The first week of her music academy should have been the most exciting, and in some ways it was. Time with her students fled quickly, but she didn't have nearly enough of them to fill her days. With school out and no studies to tend to, hours between music lessons crept by.

Deborah's disappearance continued to haunt Caroline. Her room was too empty with her cousin gone. And with no news forthcoming from the Pinkertons, concern for Deborah's safety and circumstances increased daily.

But the most troublesome aspect of summer was that Caroline no longer saw Joshua regularly. In fact, she hadn't seen him at all since Saturday afternoon when she'd taken her stand against his card-playing habit. Hours between students had allowed ample opportunity for wondering whether he'd kept his distance because of her criticism of skat, or because he was busy at his father's store. Each ring of the phone had brought hope that he was on the other end of the line wanting permission to call on her as he had claimed the night before graduation. But no such call had been received.

She was wondering whether he would attend the strawberry social tonight when her thoughts were interrupted by the sound of Vida approaching.

"It is hot, no?" She waved her apron, fanning herself.

"Yes, very hot," Caroline replied, unable to work up sufficient energy to return the smile Vida offered.

"Vat is wrong?"

Caroline shrugged, unwilling to explain.

"You miss *Fraulein* Deborah."

Caroline nodded.

"And young Mr. Bolden . . . vat trouble goes there?"

Caroline was struggling for a simple explanation when

Vida continued.

"Each one knows best where his own shoe pinches."

Caroline was pondering the meaning of the proverb when Vida spoke again.

"Those who don't pick roses in summer, vill not pick them in vinter, either." With those words, she returned to the kitchen.

Caroline pondered the proverb only moments before retrieving her parasol from the front hall and setting a course for Bolden & Sons Furniture and Hardware.

CHAPTER

9

Caroline wasn't sure what she would say to Joshua when she saw him. She was only certain that she longed to be with him. The door of Bolden & Sons was wide open when she arrived, but Joshua was not in sight. Zimri, busy with a customer in the hardware department, acknowledged her presence with a promise to be with her shortly. She browsed in the furniture department, praying for the right words to say to Joshua. She was again admiring the oak leaf etchings on the two-drawer cabinet when he emerged from the back room, his confident stride carrying him toward her.

"Caroline," he began, arms crossed on chest. He was intending to defend his card-playing habit when a trace of her orange blossom essence, and the genuinely contrite look in her dark eyes began to melt his heart.

Seeing his determined look soften like frozen custard in the summer sun, she offered a tentative smile. "It's a fine day for a strawberry social, isn't it?"

He was still trying to puzzle out a reply when she continued.

"You're going, aren't you? To the strawberry social tonight at Solon's? His father invited the whole congregation last Sunday during church service."

"I ... uh ... "

"If I don't see you there, I just wanted you to know that ... " she paused to swallow, gathering all the sincerity she could muster for her next words, "that I wish you well at the skat conference."

Joshua watched in stunned silence as she headed out the door, his thoughts confused, his feet rooted to the floor. Though his heart said to go after her, she had slipped out of the store and down the street before he managed to act on the impulse. But she was all the way down Center Street, turning onto Lake by the time he stepped outside.

Caroline couldn't help feeling disappointed that her effort to mend the rift with Joshua had proved less than successful. She would go to the strawberry social, anyway. At least it would fill a few hours in a pleasurable and innocent pursuit, and give her mother an opportunity to get out of the house now that Roxana had improved sufficiently to return to Grand Rapids.

Caroline was coming through the foyer when she heard her mother on the telephone in the parlor.

"I'll tell her as soon as she comes in. Good-bye, Joshua."

"I'm home, Mother!" Caroline called, stashing her parasol in the hall tree stand.

Ottilia emerged from the parlor. "That was Joshua. He asked me to tell you he'll come calling at seven to take you to the strawberry social at Solon's. You're to ring him up if there's any change."

Torn between outrage at his presumption, and thankfulness for his attention, she headed for the stairs. "I'm going to look for something cooler to wear."

"Don't be long. Vida has dinner almost ready."

Caroline searched her own closet, then Deborah's for an appropriate ensemble, finally settling on a pink silk blouse waist her cousin had left behind, and her own narrow white skirt with a flared hem. Much to her—and her mother's—surprise, her father arrived home in time for dinner at six, promising her mother an evening out at the social.

The door knocker sounded at seven and Caroline answered to find Joshua looking fresher and cooler than the hot summer day would imply. His suit, the grey flannel one, sported a daisy in the buttonhole that gave him a summery, casual appearance. His hair was neatly parted on the side and dressed with a pleasant-smelling tonic, the slick look maturing his youthful countenance. The only hint of whimsy was on the straw boater he held in his hand. Tucked into the grey hat band was a trio of small orange feathers.

The sight of Caroline was like a breath of fresh air to Joshua. Just looking at her, in her pale strawberry blouse and white linen skirt, reminded him of the berries and cream he hankered for. His moment of refreshment was short-lived, however, for Caroline's father was soon there to greet him, too.

"Come in, lad. Hope you don't mind if Mrs. Chappell and I tag along with you young folks. She'll be ready in a minute. I'll go see if I can speed her along."

Alone in the foyer with Caroline, he pondered a plan he'd come up with since she'd left the store—a plan to spend time with her after his trip to Detroit—but he couldn't bring it up yet. He tried to think of something else to say. The only words coming to mind were far from appropriate —that she looked as delicious as a plate of strawberries and cream. He was still searching for an alternative when she offered a question.

"Will you be wearing that suit to the skat conference? It gives you presence."

"Then I suppose I should," he replied, fidgeting with his hat. "I like the way you look tonight . . . all summery and cool."

She smiled, her gaze shifting to the lacy gloves on the hall table. As she reached for them and started pulling them on, a question came to Joshua's mind.

"Have you heard from your cousin?"

"Not a word."

"Nothing from the Pinkertons in Detroit?"

"Nor Cleveland. Mother insisted on hiring them to look there, too. She still thinks Deborah followed Taman there."

The subject was forgotten when her folks joined them, leading the way along Lake Street toward Solon's house at the corner of Emmons. Joshua couldn't have felt prouder if he'd won an automobile at the skat conference, having Caroline at his side, her hand tucked into the crook of his arm.

At the social, they all sat at the table where his folks were seated. Zimri and Solon were with them, too. When Joshua exchanged glances with them, he could see that they were jealous. Solon had already confided that he'd have invited Deborah, if she hadn't run off. And Zimri had his eye on a young lady from up north who was in town visiting the Graybiels, but he hadn't gotten up the nerve to invite her to the social.

The thought was derailed by the sound of Caroline's laugh. Joshua particularly liked its distinctive rhythm. It sounded a lot like her mama's, and the way the two of them were teasing each other and Mr. Chappell, it seemed as if he were keeping company with a flock of happy woodpeckers. It was a sweet sound he could listen to for the rest of his life—sweeter, even, than the strawberries and cream served up by Solon's mother.

But Mrs. Chappell suddenly grew grim, her frosty gaze on someone approaching from behind. When Joshua turned to see who it was, he almost choked on the strawberry he was swallowing.

There, big as life, was Neal Taman.

Without even excusing herself, Mrs. Chappell was on her feet and face to face with the outsider.

"Mr. Taman, a lot of nerve you have, showing your face in this town again!"

Mr. Chappell rose to join them, along with Joshua and Caroline.

Taman tipped his straw hat, his smile fading. "Begging your pardon, Mrs. Chappell—"

"Begging pardon will get you nowhere with me, Mr. Taman. You put my niece to work on your stage after I expressly forbid it, didn't you?"

He shook his head. "That's simply not true."

"Don't add lying to your other sins, Mr. Taman!" she warned.

Mr. Chappell lay his hand on his wife's shoulder. "Calm yourself, Ottilia. We haven't any proof that Deborah is in Mr. Taman's employ." To Taman, he said, "My niece ran off a week ago Friday."

Caroline said, "She left a somewhat cryptic note in my autograph book that she had decided to follow her dream." Joshua explained further. "Mrs. Chappell assumed that Deborah went after the job in your theater in Cleveland."

Taman drew a breath and smiled. "You can lay that notion to rest. I haven't seen Miss Dapprich since the night we went up in the balloon."

Charles patted his wife's shoulder. "You see, Ottilia, she's not in Cleveland after all."

Caroline regarded Taman skeptically. "Did Deborah mention to you any plan to leave Caledonia?"

He thought a moment, then shook his head. "No. Not after Mrs. Chappell put the nix on my offer of the position in Cleveland. I *do* recall talk of her mother's stage career in Detroit, and some people she knew who were connected with the theater there."

Charles said, "I've hired Pinkertons to look for her in Detroit. It's just a matter of time before they find her."

Observing Taman closely, Caroline noticed that at the mention of Pinkertons, his jaw flinched. But he covered the reaction quickly with a hopeful smile. "I'm sure she'll be back home with you in a matter of days. Now, if you'll excuse me, I think I'll try a plate of strawberries and cream."

He parted company, finding a seat with the Graybiels, Tess Johnson, and their out-of-town guest. Joshua could see the look of envy in Zimri's eye as he watched the ease with which Taman moved in. But Joshua's attention was soon on Caroline once again, her laughter rippling through the air in response to a joke her father told about a lawyer's lawyer who had five daughters and named every one of them Sue.

The strawberry social passed more quickly than a hand of skat. As Joshua left with Caroline and her folks, he was glad that Mr. Chappell suggested a stroll down to Church Street before going home, because the evening was coming to an end all too soon. Hand in his pocket, Joshua fingered the tattered ace of diamonds and his train ticket. Within hours he'd be boarding the early morning train bound for Detroit. Then it hit him. He'd rather spend the time with Caroline, engaged in a Saturday night game of Travel or Authors, or perhaps checkers or dominoes. The tempting thought was sidetracked by Mrs. Chappell's comment to her husband as they neared Church Street.

"I think I'll go home and pack. I can be in Detroit by tomorrow night."

Caroline said, "I'll go with you, Mother."

Charles laughed. "No need for either of you to go gallivanting off to Detroit, unescorted, to look for Deborah. That's what I'm paying the Pinkertons for."

Ottilia waved off the statement. "They don't know her like I do. I'm the one who went over there to rescue her back in April when her mother died. I know where to look for her. Better still, I know exactly what she looks like."

"That was different," Charles argued. "You had to see to your sister's burial."

"Papa, let Mother and me go, now that we know where Deborah is," Caroline suggested.

Charles paused at the corner of Church Street. Turning to face Caroline, he put an arm about her, the other, still wrapped about his wife's narrow waist. "Caroline, you have students to teach. We've been through this before." Pulling his wife closer, he said, "Ottilia, I don't want you leaving town. Not now."

"And why not?" Ottilia asked archly.

He grinned mischievously. "Because I need you here. I'll explain later. Now, case closed on the argument for going off to Detroit."

Joshua spoke up. "Sir, I'll be leaving for Detroit tomorrow. I'll be glad to—"

Caroline cut in. "See, Papa? Joshua's going to Detroit, too. He won't mind looking out for us on the train."

Fighting an urge to clap his hand over Caroline's mouth, Joshua said, "That wasn't what I meant, Mr. Chappell. I'll look for Deborah after the skat conference, if you'd like."

"That's mighty generous of you, son, but no need." Gazing north down Church Street, he said, "Now, like I told you before, there'll be no more talk of Detroit. On such a pleasant evening as this, we should all go down to the lake and take a ride in the rowboat. It's been sadly neglected since the Sutherland case came along. It's high time we make some use of it."

Passing the Co-operative Farmers Butter & Cheese Company, he led them down the fire lane to Emmons Lake, so peaceful and quiet nestled between cornfields on the edge of town and the village proper. It seemed especially delightful this night. Joshua wasn't sure whether it was the beauty of the sunset painting pale streaks of orange across the dusky sky, the harmony of Caroline's and her mother's voices as they sang round after round of *Row, Row, Row Your Boat*, or simply the nearness of the young lady sitting beside him on the rear seat of the rowboat. He suspected it was the closeness of Caroline, her enthusiasm for good, old-fashioned fun, and her genuinely guileless nature.

When Mr. Chappell lit into a hardy rendition of *Meet*

Me In St. Louis, Joshua willingly lent his voice to the occasion. It carried across the still waters of the lake, all but drowning out the descant notes from Caroline and her mother in a sort of contest of voices. The outing on the lake concluded as darkness settled in, and the walk home was accomplished with considerably more decorum-- excepting the bad riddles, puns, and jokes Mr. Chappell shared amidst complaints from his wife and daughter.

When they reached the front porch, Ottilia would have taken a seat in her favorite wicker chair, except for her husband's intervention. His arm about her waist, he guided her to the door.

"Now, dear, it's time we head inside. Let the young people stay out a bit longer and enjoy a little privacy." Ushering his wife through the door, he offered these last words to Joshua. "Don't stay too long, son. Tomorrow comes early."

"I'll only stay a few minutes, sir," Joshua replied, almost wishing he didn't have to board the 5:40 AM train.

When the front door had closed behind her father, Caroline chuckled. "That's Papa's way of saying he trusts you alone with me." She took a place on the wicker love seat.

Joshua joined her there, a tranquil evening chorus of crickets and roosting sparrows filling the silence between them. His mind, however, was anything but quiet. Time was short. His heart was full. He struggled to voice his thoughts. "Caroline," he began, then paused to take her hand in his. Gazing into the brown eyes that regarded him with expectation, he began again. "Caroline, I . . . do you remember the first time I came here to practice your trumpet duet?"

She visibly shuddered. "It was a very cold day in January, as I recall."

"It was cold," he allowed, "but I didn't notice."

As Caroline's gaze searched Joshua's, a warmth spread through her that had nothing at all to do with the June temperature. It had begun with the touch of his hand, spurred on by the simple meaning of his quiet words, and a tenderness in his blue eyes that she hadn't seen before.

Joshua continued, his heart at *tempo allegro*. "That first time we practiced, I . . . started to grow fond of you. And my fondness . . . "

In the awkward silence, Caroline searched for appropriate words to put him at ease. "My fondness for you, Joshua, is like a never-ending song, growing with each new verse." She didn't tell him the song had begun playing within her during their first year of high school—*pianissimo* at first —slowly gaining volume until it sometimes seemed to reach *fortissimo*.

Her admission set Joshua's heart to pounding like a big bass drum. He waited for the beat to fade, then spoke again. "I reckon we're playing the same tune where our feelings are concerned."

She squeezed his hand. "I reckon we are."

In the few bars' silence that followed, Joshua realized he was going to miss Caroline something fierce these next few days. But he wasn't ready to tell her so. Not yet.

Caroline wished Joshua wasn't going away. She'd yearn to be with him every minute when she wasn't teaching her students. But she wasn't prepared to admit it. She spoke instead of a musical composition taking shape in her mind. "I'm going to begin writing a trumpet solo while you're gone—one with organ accompaniment. Will you perform it with me in church this summer when Mrs. Barber is away?"

"Of course," he replied, flattered that she would honor him once more with her talent for musical composition. Such talk brought again to mind a plan he'd come up with since she'd left the store. "Caroline, I was wondering if . . ." In the distance he heard the 10:15 train approaching. The hour was growing late. He'd promised Mr. Chappell he wouldn't stay long. He spoke his piece. "I wondered if you'd like to go with me to a concert at St. Cecilia's sometime?"

Joshua's mention of the Grand Rapids auditorium sparked immediate interest. St. Cecilia's brought in the best musicians of the day, Caroline knew. But the train schedule what it was, they'd be extremely late coming home, not arriving in Caledonia until a quarter past one in the morning. An idea struck her, words pouring out. "We could go to the concert, then stay over with Parker and Roxana and catch a train home the next day. I'm sure they wouldn't mind, and it would be so much better than taking the night train at 12:30 from Grand Rapids."

"You're probably right," Joshua said, releasing her hand to rise. "We'll talk about it again when I get back from Detroit." Bounding off the porch, he tossed back his fawn-colored hair as he turned to wave. "See you in a few days, Caroline!"

"Godspeed," she replied, silently praying for traveling mercies. She watched him until losing sight of him on Lake Street, then headed inside.

Her father must have heard the door close, for he called to her from the parlor. "Caroline, would you please come in here? Your mother and I would like to talk to you."

96

"Coming, Papa," she replied, hoping her folks weren't going to complain that she and Joshua had stayed out too long. They were seated on the sofa, and she took the chair beside it.

Her father spoke first, a mysterious smile on his face. "Caroline, I was just telling your mother that, starting tomorrow, we'll be putting up a house guest for awhile." He lifted the lid of the crystal candy dish on the table in front of him and popped a lime gumdrop into his mouth.

Caroline stole an orange one before he replaced the lid, savoring its sweet, granular consistency as she waited for him to continue.

Her mother spoke instead, her eyes alight. "You'll never guess who's coming, Caroline."

She swallowed the last of her candy. "Great-aunt Luella?" She named her father's aunt from up north, of whom the whole family was particularly fond, but hadn't seen for the last two years.

Her father chuckled. "Not Aunt Luella, although we should write and invite her to come again."

Ottilia placed a hand on her husband's arm. "You're right, Charles. We *should* invite Aunt Luella. She's turned down our last three invitations, it's high time she agreed to a visit."

"Mother, Papa, if it's not Aunt Luella we're expecting this weekend, then who?" Caroline asked impatiently.

Her father's enigmatic smile returned. "Guess again."

Caroline sighed. "Is it a relative?"

In unison, her parents shook their heads.

Caroline grew thoughtful. "I can't think of anyone who's stayed with us in the last ten years who isn't a relative."

Her mother said, "This person used to visit us all the time, but never over night."

Her father added, "You haven't seen this person for a good long time."

Frustrated, Caroline said, "Santa Clause?"

"Ho, ho, ho!" her father boomed. "Amusing, you are—but incorrect."

Her mother said, "This individual is considerably younger than jolly old Saint Nick."

Her father said, "I'll give you a hint." He cradled his arms, moving back and forth as if rocking a baby.

Caroline drew an impatient breath. "You're not making any sense. The only babies I know are relatives, and I've seen all of them within the last few weeks."

Her mother went into the front hall, returning with a polished Petoskey stone the size of a fist from the curio cabinet while her father kept up the rocking motion.

Putting the two together, Caroline guessed, "Rock?"

Her folks nodded vigorously. Then her father pretended he were grasping an imaginary handle, moving it up and down with effort.

"Pump. Rock-pump. It doesn't make sense," Caroline concluded.

Her father pretended to catch water in cupped hands, then splash it on his face.

"Well?" Caroline asked. Then it hit her. "The Rockwells are coming!" They'd lived next door before the Chappells moved to Caledonia ten years ago.

Her father shook his head, holding up one finger.

"One of the Rockwells is coming," she surmised, guessing, "Tommy?"

"Yes!" her folks confirmed in unison.

"He's coming here?" she asked in disbelief, wondering what the fair-haired playmate of her youth looked like now that he was all grown up.

"Tommy will be here on the one o'clock train tomorrow afternoon," her father informed her. "He's recently graduated from Olivet College."

"Graduated from college already?" Caroline asked, knowing Tommy was only two years older than herself.

"He skipped a grade in school, and finished his four-year degree in three years," her father explained.

Her mother said, "He's coming to talk to your father about clerking in his law firm."

Her father continued. "You know how busy we've been. When Tommy's father looked me up on his way through Grand Rapids last week, I asked what his boy was doing, and when he said Tommy was looking for a position, I suggested that he consider coming to work for me."

Caroline's head moved from side to side as she took in all that her folks were saying. Reminiscences of her earliest acquaintance with the piano emerging, she said, "I wonder if he remembers the duet we used to play—*Polly Wolly Doodle*?"

Her father checked his timepiece. "About fourteen hours from now, you'll be able to ask him yourself. Now, if you ladies will excuse me, tomorrow comes early. I'm going to turn in." He leaned over to peck Ottilia on the cheek, then rose.

Ottilia rose, too. "I'll be up as soon as I tell Vida about our house guest. Good night, Caroline."

"Good night, Mother. Good night, Papa." When they had gone, she wandered into the music room and folded back the keyboard cover, thoughts drifting to the past when

99

she was six years old and Tommy was eight. Her own folks didn't have a piano then, but Tommy had taught her some very simple tunes on the Rockwells' upright. Taking a seat on the bench, she plunked out the tune to *Polly Wolly Doodle"*, one-finger fashion as she had done so many years ago. In her mind, she could picture Tommy clearly, and hear him playing the bass notes in accompaniment. But ten years had passed since she'd last seen him. Was he still the fair-haired, musically inclined prankster and tease of his youth?

CHAPTER

10

"Carolina!"

Caroline immediately recognized Tommy's corruption of her name and his shrill whistle which followed, but the voice, and its owner—the tall, strapping young man with a mustache who waved and hurried toward her just outside the Caledonia Station—bore little resemblance to the boy she remembered.

"Tommy!" she cried, falling victim to a hug that crushed her cheek against his firm, broad chest and sent a whiff of clove into her nostrils, reminding her of his breath-freshening habit of chewing on clove studs.

The scent dissipated as he put her away from him, hands on her shoulders, and studied her with sparkling blue eyes. Gradually, a crooked smile tilted the right half of his mustache. "You're a sight to behold, Carolina! A sight to behold!"

"I can hardly believe it's you, Tommy!"

"Well, I can believe it's *you*, Carolina. You've still got that curly dark hair, that tiny little waist—I'd have known you anywhere!"

Caroline could feel her face warming beneath his gaze,

and was glad when her mother spoke up.

"Good to see you, Tommy. Welcome to Caledonia."

"Thank you Mrs. Chappell." He paused in his scrutiny long enough to shake her hand, his focus again on Caroline. "By gum, there's something I almost forgot." Digging into his jacket pocket, he extracted a crumpled paper sack and thrust it into her hands. "For you, Carolina."

She hastily opened it, discovering several orange gumdrops inside. Immediately, she popped one into her mouth, chewing as she exclaimed, "My favorites! You remembered!"

"Of course I remembered!"

She offered gumdrops to her mother and Tommy. When he refused, she said, "Don't you like gumdrops anymore?"

"Like them?" he repeated incredulously, "I started out with a pound, and ate all but the orange ones on the train!"

Ottilia gasped. "Shame on you, Tommy. Don't you have a bellyache?"

Placing his hand on the area in question, he thought a moment, his gaze again on Caroline. "If I did, it's gone now, chased away by the sight of Carolina." He offered a broad grin.

Growing self-conscious beneath his scrutiny, Caroline said, "You're a sight to behold, yourself, Tommy Rockwell. Now, come along and let us show you your lodgings." Turning about, she pointed to her home, easily visible a block away. "That's our destination."

Tommy's eyes widened. "That big white place down the way? I had no idea you were living in a palace. That's a tad fancy for plain old Tommy Rockwell, don't you think, Princess Carolina?"

She let loose her staccato laugh.

Tommy laughed, too, his booming chuckle the bass counterpart to hers.

She spoke again. "Tommy Rockwell, you're neither plain, nor old, and I'm most certainly *not* a princess. Now come along. We've got a lot of catching up to do."

From the moment Tommy set foot on the front walk, he complimented effusively the grand new home that had been completed only seven months earlier. Each room he viewed received his praise. Caroline was especially gratified when they reached the music room and he sat down on the piano bench to strike out the bass chords to *Polly Wolly Doodle*. She quickly joined him. One duet led to another until they had reached the limits of Tommy's repertoire and expertise. Although his piano playing had improved considerably since he was eight, it fell far short of Caroline's ability, and for an hour, he listened to the private recital she offered, applauding heartily after each piece.

The heat of the day was becoming oppressive, so they moved onto the front porch, talking over old times while sipping ice-cold lemonade. His trunk was delivered from the station at four, and when he had stowed it in his room, he asked Caroline if there were any watering holes nearby fit for swimming. When she suggested Emmons Lake, he immediately talked her into going for a swim.

"It'll be like the good old days, before you moved, only this time, you're old enough to go in the water!" he commented, referring to her childhood days before she learned to swim. Then, she would sit on the bank, often with Deborah, and watch with great envy while Tommy, Parker, and several other neighbor children frolicked in the pond.

When they had dressed in their bathing togs and were nearing the lake, Caroline asked Tommy, "Do you remember my cousin, Deborah, who used to stay with us from time to time when I was little?"

"Sure do! A bit of a rascal. Had a passion for butterflies, as I recall."

"She's still a rascal, and still loves butterflies," Caroline confirmed. "She came to live with us again in April, then ran off the night we graduated from high school."

"That sounds like the Deborah I remember." Setting his towel on the bank, he said, "Race you to the other side!"

Caroline ran into the water after him, pushing off the muddy bottom in a race that left her far behind by the time she'd returned to the shore. Tommy was ready and waiting, pushing her under in a strictly playful spirit, grabbing her by the ankle when she tried to escape, kicking up a spray of water that refracted into miniature prisms in the late afternoon sunlight. The outing was almost like those of twelve years ago, except today she was in the midst of the activity and enjoying every droplet of water sent her way. Before heading home, they took a row around the lake, doing more catching up on school days lived apart while their swim suits dried in the warm sun. Tommy told of the broken arm he'd suffered falling out of an apple tree at age twelve, the baseball team he'd pitched for after making a full recovery, and the collision he'd gotten into as a fifteen-year-old driving a brand new horse and buggy his father had purchased.

"I didn't get hurt, but I had to go to work for two years on the Franklin farm to pay the damages," he explained. "I didn't think I'd ever work my way out from under that debt. Worst of all, I had to give up baseball to help with the planting and harvesting."

Caroline smiled. "But that's all behind you. Now, you're a college graduate ready to take the world by storm!"

Tommy chuckled. "Maybe not the world, but at least the Chappell law firm. Which reminds me, it's time we head back. Your father will be home for dinner soon, and we've got some washing up to do before we dress for dinner."

Purchasing a Grand Rapids newspaper on the way home, he went straight upstairs to his room, emerging upon the arrival of her father who came from the city on the 7:25 train. Dinner table conversation centered on Tommy's college course in liberal arts, and the Sutherland case which had kept Caroline's father occupied for weeks. When the gentlemen moved to the front porch to discuss the duties Tommy would be expected to perform if employed at the law firm, Caroline adjourned to the music room.

There, she prepared assignments for Tess Johnson and the other piano students who would be coming for their second lesson starting Monday. When she ran out of staff paper, she searched for more in the piano bench, coming across the music to the trumpet duet she had composed for her recital. With a start, she realized that since Tommy's arrival, she hadn't given one thought to Joshua, nor had she composed a single note of the trumpet solo she had promised to write while he was gone. Hurriedly finishing the simple tunes for her students, she set a clean sheet of staff paper on the music rack. Staring down at the keyboard, she waited for inspiration to come regarding the introduction to his solo. Striking one chord, then another, she struggled to find a pleasing progression, a melodious motif, a riveting rhythm. But the sounds of laughter filtering in from the front porch seemed to screen out musical inspiration, making her toss pencil and staff paper half-filled with cross-outs into the piano bench. No sooner had the lid banged shut, than her mother appeared at the door.

"No success with your composing?"

Caroline sighed. "I can't seem to concentrate."

Arm about her daughter's shoulders, Ottilia guided her toward the front porch, saying, "From the sounds of it, your father and Tommy are finished discussing the terms of his employment and due for some feminine company."

Taking a seat beside her mother on the front porch swing, Caroline listened with interest to Tommy's descriptions of college life—a professor who came to class every day for two years wearing the exact same tattered plaid jacket; his complete lack of response when three female coeds secretly switched it with a brand new one; the long semester Tommy spent on probation for allowing his grades to slip during his first year.

"Thank goodness that's all in the past," he concluded. "On a different note—forgive the pun—I was reading a notice in the Grand Rapids newspaper about a piano recital to be held tomorrow evening at an auditorium called Saint something-or-other."

Caroline spoke up. "St. Cecilia's?"

"That's right," Tommy confirmed. "I thought it would be interesting to hear—"

Charles cut in. "Let's all go. I'll treat everyone to dinner at the Pantlind Hotel first, then we'll take in the recital." His gaze on Ottilia, he added, "Unless you have other plans, my dear?"

Ottilia smiled. "If I did, I'd cancel them for the chance

to go out with my husband for only the second time in . . . how many months has it been since you took on the Sutherland case?"

"Then it's all set," Charles concluded. "Tommy and I are taking the early train to the city tomorrow morning to work in my office, but you ladies could take the one o'-clock train. After the recital, we can come back on the 12:30 train . . . or maybe I should make reservations at the Pantlind to stay over. That way we could take some time after church on Sunday to show Tommy around the city."

Ottilia chuckled. "Your plan is sounding better all the time."

Caroline spoke up. "Papa, do you suppose we could attend services at Fountain Street Church? I love listening to their organ, and looking at their stained glass windows."

"Fountain Street Church, it is," he said, slapping his knee.

Her mother said, "I wonder if Parker and Roxana would like to hear the recital, too?"

Charles said, "I'll ring up Roxana and invite them as soon as we get to the office. Then, I'll reserve seats at St. Cecilia's and rooms at the Pantlind." Rising, he added, "Now, I'd best turn in, or I'll never make it up in time for the 5:40 train."

CHAPTER

11

Detroit, Michigan

At the awards dinner Sunday night, Joshua gazed across the roomful of eight hundred competitors as he reflected on his two days at the skat conference. He'd sorely underestimated the level of skill and experience he'd encountered. But he was glad he'd come. He wouldn't be driving home in a brand new automobile, but he could return a winner if he discovered Deborah's whereabouts. Tomorrow, he'd make inquiries, and he prayed they'd pay off. By staying over the extra day, he'd get home too late to make the Independence Day band performance, an absence Professor Neron would never tolerate. Like it or not, Joshua would be out of the band.

On his way to breakfast he bought the latest edition of the newspaper, intending to plan a search strategy over a plateful of thick waffles heaped with fresh strawberries and topped with a generous dollop of whipped cream. As he dug into his first forkful, he realized he could get used to this kind of luxury—the thick carpet beneath his feet; a velvet-covered cushion padding his seat; the fancy white table linens spread out before him. But his favorite aspect of the dining room was its wide view of the busy city street.

Watching streetcars come and go, he marveled at the number of private and commercial vehicles that were causing congestion. The ice wagon with its big rear step paused to make a delivery across the street. A coal wagon tried to pull around, bringing traffic from the opposite direction to a temporary halt. Then a greengrocer's cart nearly went out of control when a horseless carriage passed by, its chugging and popping sounds spooking the horses.

Downing the last forkful of waffles, he realized he hadn't even opened up his newspaper. Turning to the entertainment section, he studied the theater notices. Mary Hampton was the main feature of a vaudeville program called *The Melodrama* at the Temple Theater. The description, " . . . small doses of light and serious work and the introduction of vocal and instrumental music . . . " made Joshua think it would be a magnet for the likes of Deborah. Reading on, the Avenue Theater's offering sounded equally enticing. "*Pousse Cafe* is replete with jingling music, pretty dances and scenic attractiveness." With fifty people in the company and the chorus, Deborah could have found a position there. But he couldn't rule out the possibility that she had landed a part with the Whitney Theater's summer stock, where *Knobs o' Tennessee* was the week's play. Newspaper in tow, he set out for the Temple Theater first.

When he arrived at a few minutes past ten, he found the place locked up tight. He pounded on the stage door to no avail. Not even a caretaker could be roused. The sign posted out front stated that the next performance would begin at eight that evening. Discouraged, he went on to the

Avenue Theater, encountering the same situation. Tempted to give up his search, he headed for the Whitney Theater, anyway. There, he found a rehearsal in progress, and slipped into the front row to wait for an opportunity to inquire about Caroline's cousin. He hadn't been there long when an elderly fellow pushing a wide dust mop approached him.

"If you're lookin' to join summer stock, young man, it's my understandin' that the positions are all filled up."

Joshua shook his head. "I'm not an actor. I'm looking for a young lady by the name of Dapprich—Deborah Dapprich. Ever heard of her?"

The old man's eyes lit up, a smile carving new wrinkles in his wizened chin as he leaned, stooped-shouldered, on his mop handle. "Heard of her? I've known her since she was a babe in arms! Knew her mother, Miss Emeline, too."

"Have you seen Deborah recently?" Joshua asked eagerly.

The old man nodded. "Now that she's all growed up, she's sure got herself a followin'. You're the third fella to come lookin' for her in the last week!"

CHAPTER

12

Caledonia, Michigan

As Caroline prepared for the arrival of Tess Johnson bright and early Monday morning, she reflected on how the piano performance at St. Cecilia's hadn't been quite what she'd expected. It had been entertaining, nonetheless, and Sunday's church service and tour of the city with her folks and Tommy had been enjoyable, as well.

At the sound of the door knocker, she invited Tess into the music room, discovering to her delight that the young girl had practiced her assignment, learning each note to perfection. Her delivery was somewhat stiff and mechanical, however, in need of variations from her *forte* volume, and a smoother rhythm. Caroline spent the first half-hour getting Tess to curve her fingers properly over the keys and inject feeling into the melodies, then they went over the new pieces Tess would practice for her next lesson. At the end of the hour, as Tess gathered her music together, she spoke to Caroline with an air of confidentiality.

"Ya know that Mr. Taman fella who was at the strawberry social?"

Caroline nodded.

"Well, he done offered me a position in his bank over in Cleveland. Said I'd make a whole lot more money there than workin' for Mrs. Graybiel, but I turned him down cold. Don't know when I'd ever get to see my granny down in Middleville. 'Sides, I'd have to give up my pie-anna lessons, and I ain't about to do that!"

"I'm glad you're staying," Caroline told her as they walked together to the front door. "I'll see you next week, same time."

"I'll be here!" Tess promised, nearly missing a step as she hurried off the front porch.

As Caroline watched the girl head around the bend to Johnson Street, she couldn't understand why Taman would try to hire such a rough-cut gem. Logic eluding her, she turned her attention to her next student, now coming up the walk.

By dinner time, Caroline was quite hungry and fatigued. She had worked extra hard that afternoon teaching two Tuesday students so as to avoid conflicts with the Independence Day celebration. In addition, the evening meal had been postponed until half past seven in order to accommodate the arrival of her father and Tommy on the 7:25 train. All evening, Caroline held out hope that Joshua would come by, or at least ring her up saying he had returned from Detroit, but the phone didn't ring. As she climbed the stairs to turn in, she could hear the 10:15 train rolling to a stop. She was tempted to run back downstairs and up the street to see if he was on it, but she refrained, still wondering how he'd made out at the skat conference when her head hit the pillow.

A good night's sleep restored her energy, and thoughts of Joshua were eclipsed by Tommy's enthusiasm to participate in the activities scheduled for the Independence Day celebration on Center Street. With not a rain cloud in sight, the hot sun burned down upon them as she and her folks watched the noon parade. High-wheelers headed the procession, ridden by the Beelers, whose father owned the drug store. Behind them came the Caledonia Band playing *Stars and Stripes Forever*. It was then—when the band went by—that Caroline felt certain Joshua had won an automobile at the skat conference, for he wasn't performing in the band, and she couldn't imagine him giving up his membership for anything less.

Again, thoughts of Joshua were overridden by the activities on Center Street when Tommy insisted she enter the sack race. Hopping over the finish line just behind Tess, she tossed sack aside to watch Tommy in the slow bicycle race. He lagged behind Zimri by mere inches, earning himself a shiny new silver dollar for coming in last.

Afterward, they joined the crowds gathered at the bowery, a bandstand covered with branches which had been constructed in front of the drug store and grocery. There, Caroline, Tommy, and her folks listened to Village President, Elmer Hale, give a speech about the patriotic spirit of the nation's founders which was still very much alive in the village. When the one o'clock train from the East came through, momentarily interrupting, Caroline didn't give a thought to Joshua being on it, so certain was she that he was making his way home upon the seat of a brand new motor car. When Mr. Hale had finished his speech, Caroline's father bought four glasses of red lemonade from the Van Amburg sisters who were serving refreshments on the sidewalk in front of their shop.

Her mother drank eagerly from her glass, patting her forehead with her handkerchief. "This heat is absolutely making me wilt. When I've finished my lemonade, I'm going home to sit on the porch."

No sooner had she spoken than the Clemens orchestra struck up a waltz. Charles put his hand affectionately on her shoulder. "Promise me one dance, dear, then I'll go home, too." Seeing reluctance in her speculative gaze, he added, "You owe it to yourself, since you missed the Summer Reception."

Finishing her lemonade, Ottilia set her glass aside, accepting the arm her husband offered. "One waltz, then home we go," she said.

As they joined the other waltzing couples, Tommy turned to Caroline. "What do you say, Carolina? Take a turn around the dance floor—I mean, street?"

With a nod, she found herself being led at a proper arm's length around the dirt floor. Tommy, though taller by a good twelve inches, was an able partner, accomplished and graceful in his movements. When the waltz ended and her folks had taken their leave, she gladly danced with Tommy again. The piece was coming to an end when she noticed Neal Taman at the sidelines. His gaze, so obviously focused on her, made her uncomfortable.

Taman knew he should have stayed on the train and passed through Caledonia, but he couldn't get Caroline Chappell out of his mind. Overcome by an uncontrollable urge to see her once again, he'd stepped off the 5:40 AM train on impulse, waiting patiently throughout the morning for the festivities which were sure to draw the Chappell girl to Center Street. Remaining in the shadows, he had expected her to appear with the younger Bolden brother. He was surprised to see her with some tall, blond fellow, instead, no Joshua in sight.

Biding his time until Caroline's folks had gone home, Taman began making his way toward her, jealousy rising within. By the time the third dance started, he was at her side. Hand outstretched, a smile fixed in place, he spoke as warmly as possible.

"Miss Chappell, may I have the pleasure of this dance?"

His velvety tone, warm as the July day, couldn't melt the iciness in his blue eyes. Caroline wanted to decline, but Tommy stepped away before she could respond, saying, "Go ahead, Carolina. I'll be right over there." He tossed his head in the direction of the lemonade stand.

Taman took her hand, so small and delicate, in his, placing the other at her tiny waist. The heat of the day had intensified her orange blossom scent, increasing her allure. But apprehension creased her brow, so he made every effort to put her at ease with the choice and tone of his words. "From the looks of it, the young Mr. Bolden has competition." He nodded in Tommy's direction.

Caroline laughed stiffly. "You're mistaken. Tommy is just a childhood friend."

"Then where is your beau? I'd have thought he'd be playing with the band."

Resenting his prying, Caroline tried to put the best face on the situation, claiming, "I believe he's somewhere between here and Detroit, driving home in his new automobile." Silently, she prayed it was so.

Taman made no reply, his gaze locking on to penetrate her soul even as the heat of the sun enhanced the sickeningly sweet scent of his hair tonic. Breaking eye contact,

Caroline noticed Tess Johnson beneath the drug store awning. A thought leaped to mind, a less personal subject she introduced.

"Now it's my turn for a question, Mr. Taman. I'm wondering why you offered Tess Johnson a position at your bank. Surely you could find equally suitable prospects in Cleveland."

Taman smiled, reaching deep within for a convincing, sympathetic response. "Perhaps so, Miss Chappell, but would you fault me for trying to do a good deed?"

Flustered by his seemingly heartfelt reply, Caroline said, "No, of course not. It's just that—"

Taman went on. "I know that Tess is an orphan and that the her chances of escaping the world of the domestic are slim, indeed, until she marries. I simply thought that her prospects for both good employment and eventually, a good mate, would be better in Cleveland."

Feeling guilty for having questioned him, Caroline was about to apologize when he continued.

"I would have offered you a position, had I thought you'd accept. But you're far too dedicated to your music and your new academy. No?"

Flustered, she said, "No—I mean—yes, I'm dedicated to my music, and no, I wouldn't accept."

He chuckled. "As I suspected. Of course, if you can recommend someone else—a friend, perhaps—I'll gladly interview her."

The sincerity of his tone cast off much doubt concerning his motives. Nevertheless, Caroline was unable to fully trust him. "I can't think of anyone at present," she replied thoughtfully.

"Perhaps you will, in which case you can contact me at

the hotel. I'll be here until the 7:25 train." The music ending, he escorted her to the lemonade stand where Tommy was in conversation with the elder Bolden boy. Unwilling to release her, he seized the opportunity to spend a few more minutes in her company. "May I treat you to a glass of lemonade, Miss Chappell?"

Reluctant to accept, but in need of another cold drink, she nodded, finishing half the glass before pausing.

When the glass parted from Caroline's lips, Taman struggled to overcome a raging desire to kiss away the red mustache that so effectively enhanced her childlike, innocent nature. Trembling with lusty need, he diffused his dark passion by forcing a quiet laugh, then offering his handkerchief. "You have a ring of red lemonade about the mouth, Miss Chappell."

Though he spoke in a quiet, confidential tone, Caroline knew her cheeks were turning red, as well. Fumbling for her own handkerchief, she nearly spilled the remainder of her lemonade before Taman took it from her with a shaky hand.

The instant Caroline had put away her handkerchief, Taman returned the glass to her, saying, "Now, if you'll pardon me, I have business to attend to."

His hasty retreat, in the direction of the hotel, baffled Caroline, as did nearly every other aspect of Neal Taman. His countenance seemed to change from dark to congenial and back again on a whim. His words, though sincere in their delivery, didn't ring quite right. And the way his hand had started to tremble, she wondered if he was beset by some dreaded disease.

Such thoughts evaporated at the sound of the band striking up another tune, and Tommy's enthusiastic response.

"Drink up, Carolina! Let's dance!"

Having traveled throughout the night, a fatigued Joshua arrived on the one o'clock train and headed home to catch some sleep. By dinner time, he was feeling much better. Then Zimri began talking about Caroline and some out-of-town friend by the name of Tommy Rockwell who'd come to stay. The moment the meal was over, Joshua returned to his room, donned again his new grey summer suit, and set out for the Chappells'.

The sounds that greeted him when he reached the front walk of the Queen Ann were not what he wanted to hear. Someone was fumbling a ragtime melody on the piano—Tommy Rockwell, he presumed. But the laughter, a duet of Caroline's high staccato against a deeper chuckle Joshua didn't recognize, was far more troubling. He climbed the porch steps, knocking impatiently. Caroline answered, the stumbling rag tune still playing in the background.

"Joshua! You're back!" Peering beyond him to the street, she asked, "Where's you're automobile? You did win one, didn't you?"

Fighting the urge to hang his head, he kept his gaze steady. "No, I didn't. But I did learn something about—"

"You *didn't*?"

Regret keen, he was eager to change to a more favorable topic—his news of Deborah—when Caroline went on.

"I was so positive you'd won a motor car. I couldn't imagine another reason good enough to keep you from playing with the band today."

When he would have explained, a striking blond fellow much taller than himself appeared at her side, his hand extended in greeting. "Tommy Rockwell. You must be

Joshua. Pleased to meet you." Following a firm hand-shake, Tommy jostled Caroline's shoulder. "Carolina was just trying to teach me the *Maple Leaf Rag*. She's gone crazy for ragtime since the concert Saturday at St. Cecilia's, haven't you, Carolina?"

Joshua's heart plummeted. "You went to St. Cecilia's?"

She nodded with enthusiasm. "I wish you'd been there. We had the most wonderful time!" The look she gave Tommy was pure mischief.

He chuckled. "As in *rag*time, right Carolina?" He started toward the music room, taking her with him, his hand on her wrist. "Play a ragtime tune for Joshua. Play the *Maple Leaf*. I think I can get it if I hear it one more time."

Joshua followed, impressed by Caroline's skill with the syncopated rhythm. But as he listened to her banter with Tommy, and observed the genuine, playful affection between them, he concluded that not only had he lost at cards, he was losing at romance, as well. When she had spent five minutes—which seemed like twenty—teaching Tommy the errors of his ragtime ways, she left him alone at the piano to practice and took the chair beside his.

"Tell me about Detroit, the conference. Did you have a good time?"

Fingering the tattered ace of diamonds in his pocket, Joshua replied, "My luck ran out at cards, but I have news about your cousin."

Caroline's dark eyes widened. "You have news about Deborah?"

No sooner had he nodded than Caroline rose, hurrying toward the parlor as she called for her mother and father to join them in the music room. Tommy ceased his plunking on the piano, and with he and the Chappells giving rapt attention, Joshua told what he knew.

"I spoke with a janitor at the Whitney Theater who saw Deborah a week ago Saturday."

Ottilia turned to Charles. "You were right. She *did* go back to the people she knew in Detroit."

Joshua said, "But she was on her way to Cleveland. A fellow came to fetch her and take her there."

Caroline grew angry. "Neal Taman. The nerve—"

"No," Joshua interrupted, "the man didn't fit Taman's description, but the janitor says Deborah told him she was gonna work for Taman, and this other man was taking her the rest of the way to Cleveland."

Caroline stood abruptly. "I'm going straight to the Caledonia Hotel to confront Taman, the scoundrel!"

Ottilia gasped. "He's here? In Caledonia?"

"I danced with him this afternoon!" Caroline exclaimed as she headed for the door.

Ottilia followed.

Charles was close behind. "Ottilia, Caroline, stay put. I'll speak with Taman, but I doubt . . . " His words were drowned out by the sound of the a train leaving town.

Joshua and Tommy caught up with the Chappells in the foyer. When the train had gone, Caroline turned to the others, hands raised. "Too late. Taman said he was leaving on the 7:25 train."

Her mother sighed. "The rascal!"

A hand on her shoulder, Charles headed back to the music room. "I don't think it would have done me any good to talk with him, anyway."

"Probably not," Ottilia agreed. "And those Pinkertons

haven't been any help. They haven't done one thing to find Deborah!"

When all were seated once again, Joshua told Mrs. Chappell, "It's not entirely true, what you said about the Pinkertons. They did look for Deborah in Detroit, and they nearly found her, but the janitor told me they arrived at the Whitney Theater about an hour after she'd left."

Ottilia said, "We still haven't heard a word from the Cleveland agency. You'd think they'd have wired days ago with news that they'd located the girl."

Charles shook his head in bewilderment. "I think there's a lot more to this than we suspect. I'll contact the Cleveland folks and inquire as to the status of their search."

Pulling a small notebook and pencil from his jacket pocket, Tommy said, "I'll take care of that for you first thing when we get to the office tomorrow, sir."

"Thanks, son." Pausing to wipe his brow, Charles said, "I could do with a tall glass of Vida's Independence Day punch. How about the rest of you?"

Hearing agreement all around, Ottilia said, "I'll go help her pour."

Tucking his handkerchief in his pocket, Charles said, "I'd surely appreciate it if you ladies could serve it on the porch. It's a tad close in here."

Leading the exodus, Mr. Chappell took the latest issue of the Grand Rapids paper with him, situating himself on the swing to study its pages while Joshua joined Caroline and Tommy in comfortable wicker chairs a few feet away.

Caroline was at no loss to initiate conversation, her dark eyes sparkling as her gaze moved from Tommy to Joshua. "I wish you'd been with us at St. Cecilia's. We heard a wonderful pianist."

121

Tommy said, "I wish you'd been there, too, Joshua. Then, I'd have had someone else to share my embarrassment over Carolina's boldness."

"Embarrassment?" Caroline asked incredulously. "You were egging me on!"

"I didn't expect you to take the poor fellow by the hand and drag him back to the piano after he'd just finished an hour's performance, then force him to give you a private lesson on the art of ragtime!"

"He didn't seem to mind," Caroline claimed, "and neither did you, at the time. You were practically breathing down my neck, trying to catch every word—and note—that Mr. Joplin offered."

Joshua straightened, "Joplin? Did you say Joplin?"

Tommy nodded. "Mr. Scott Joplin was the featured performer."

Caroline added, "He's the fellow who played at—"

Joshua finished for her, "—the Louisiana Purchase Exposition last year."

Tommy said, "He's a great performer, and talented composer."

Eager to leave the topic of St. Cecilia's behind, Joshua took a new angle. "While we're on the subject of music—"

Tommy laughed. "I don't think Carolina's been off it for more than a few seconds at a time since I arrived Friday afternoon."

Caroline straightened. "What do you mean? We spent the latter part of the afternoon swimming at the lake, and didn't mention music even once!"

"I stand corrected, Carolina."

Temper rising, Joshua addressed Tommy sharply. "Her name's Caroline, not Carolina."

Tommy's brows narrowed in surprise.

Caroline spoke up, a slight edge to her voice. "Tommy's been calling me 'Carolina' ever since I can remember. I don't mind, Joshua. Really. Now what was it you were going to say about music?"

Struggling to control his pique and remember his question, Joshua paused a moment before asking, "Did you finish that trumpet solo you were going to write for me?"

Caroline's hand flew to her mouth. "I'm sorry! I haven't finished it yet. But I will."

He was ready to ask her another question when Ottilia and Vida appeared with a tray full of punch cups. They were filled with a red liquid upon which floated blueberries and marshmallows. He sipped the fruity drink—the flavor a combination of strawberry and lemonade—and waited for an opportunity to speak. His chance came when Tommy drew his chair closer to the swing to discuss business with Charles.

Sliding his own chair closer to Caroline's, he said, "I was wondering if you'd like to go to the fireworks with me later this evening?" Silently, he prayed that the Fourth of July sparks would rekindle the flame between them—one that seemed to be dying right before his eyes.

She smiled. "Of course! We'll all go together—you, me, Tommy, Mother, Papa—maybe even Vida. All right?"

"I . . . guess so," he managed, the words sticking in his throat.

And so his outing with Caroline was shared with all the others she'd mentioned. By the end of the evening, when the last explosion had faded to darkness, he knew beyond a doubt that if he were to preserve his place with Caroline, decisive action was in order. He must let her know the

123

seriousness of his intentions, and he must do it soon. Arriving back on the Chappells' front porch, when her parents would have gone inside and taken Tommy with them, he forestalled their departure with a question.

"Mr. and Mrs. Chappell, Caroline, I have something to ask. I'd like to call on you all tomorrow evening." Knowing Mr. Chappell and Tommy would likely arrive home on the 7:25 train, he suggested, "Would half-past eight be all right?"

Mrs. Chappell offered another suggestion. "Why not come at half-past seven and join us for the evening meal?"

Knowing his stomach would be too tied in knots to eat, he told her truthfully, "I'm gonna be tied up at half-past seven, but I'll be here at eight-thirty, if you'll have me."

Caroline said, "What do you mean, if we'll have you? You know you're welcome here, appointment or no."

"I'll see you tomorrow, then," Joshua replied. As he hurried off the porch and across the tracks to Lake Street, he prayed Caroline would feel as accommodating after he'd said his piece tomorrow night.

CHAPTER

13

Caroline gave little thought to Joshua's plan to come calling, except to wonder why he'd been so formal in his request. She was sitting on the porch with her folks after dinner the following evening—Tommy had gone to look at Mr. Kinsey's photograph collection—when she spotted Joshua coming down Lake Street in his grey summer suit.

"I wonder where Joshua's been. He's so dressed up," she commented casually to her mother.

"Maybe it isn't where he's been, but where he's going," Ottilia replied, a strange look in her eye.

Caroline sighed. "Just what do you mean by that?"

Her mother grinned. "Nothing, my dear. Just an idle comment."

Joshua's arrival prevented Caroline from pursuing the topic, although she was certain her mother knew more than she was saying. When she saw the strained look on

Joshua's face, her questions only multiplied. And when she heard the shakiness of his voice, she felt real pity for him.

"Mr. and Mrs. Chappell, Caroline, may I speak to you in the parlor?" Joshua was so nervous, it seemed as though a hundred musicians were playing sour notes inside his stomach.

Mr. Chappell rose, offering a casual smile as he draped a welcoming arm over Joshua's shoulders. "Come on in, son. You're practically family, after all the hours you and Caroline spent rehearsing for her recital."

Joshua made no reply, nervously fingering the tattered ace inside his pocket while praying silently that the Lord would steady his voice and supply him with the right words. The heat of the summer's night sent moisture trickling down his temple. He dabbed it with his handkerchief, then ran a finger inside a collar that seemed to grow smaller by the second. It was so tight by the time everyone had been seated in the parlor, that he thought he was about to choke.

Pausing to take each of the others in his gaze—Mr. and Mrs. Chappell on the sofa and Caroline on the love seat to his right—he rose and approached the young lady whose very presence could make the music of his heart soar to high C and beyond.

For a moment, Caroline wondered why Joshua was coming toward her with such a worried look on his face. The first whispers of an answer began to sound within when he knelt down at her feet and took both her hands in his trembling, clammy grasp.

"Caroline," he began, the *pianissimo* of his voice increasing to *mezzo forte* with his next words. "For ten years, we've known each other. First, we were just classmates. Then, you asked me to perform in your recital. Like your father said, from January on, I was like one of the family."

The blue of Joshua's eyes, so earnest yet vulnerable as he gazed into her own, sent Caroline's heart into an erratic, ragtime rhythm.

He paused, recalling the speech he'd planned, gathering the courage he needed to proceed. "But months ago, my feelings began to change. You weren't just a classmate. You weren't like family. You became the one person I know I always want to be with."

"Joshua . . . " His name was a whisper on her sweet breath.

Eager to continued before she could say more, his gaze shifted to her folks, his words tumbling out. "Mr. and Mrs. Chappell, I love your daughter. I want to marry her, with your blessings."

Mr. Chappell almost smiled. "Then you'd better ask her if *she* wants to marry *you*, son."

As Joshua spoke, his grip grew so tight, Caroline could hardly feel her fingers, but she could easily sense the excitement that unfolded like the *1812 Overture* as he spoke.

"Caroline, will you marry me? You don't have to answer tonight, but I need to know your intentions. I'll turn the second floor of Papa's store into an apartment for us. There's even room for a music studio, if you'd like."

"Joshua, this is so sudden . . . so unexpected. I . . . I love you, Joshua, but could you give me until tomorrow to think over your question?"

He kissed the back of her hands, then released them. Rising, he began to slowly back away. "Of course. I'll call on you tomorrow." Without so much as a good-bye, he

127

turned to make a swift exit out the front door, his heart pounding as he nearly ran down Lake Street toward Center.

Caroline's mind was in a whirl, thoughts racing through her head *prestissimo*.

Her father chuckled. "Orange Blossom, you'd be a real judy, as you're so fond of saying, not to accept Joshua's proposal! I've never seen a fellow so besotted with a gal as he is with you!"

Ottilia said, "A September wedding would be nice."

Twisting the gold and garnet ring around and around on her little finger, Caroline turned to her mother. "You knew he was going to propose! Why didn't you tell me!"

Ottilia shook her head. "I *didn't* know! But I *did* suspect it was coming when Joshua asked to speak with the three of us."

Caroline rose, pacing the floor as she mumbled to herself. "Marriage . . . an apartment over the store . . . " She wandered into the music room, sat down at the piano, and lit into the Bach *Toccata and Fugue* she'd played at her recital, trying to release her pent-up tensions, hoping to clear her mind. When she had finished, she played through the other piano pieces she had performed that night at the church. After the final note had died away, she stared down at the keys, then slowly closed the cover over them.

Applause sounded from the corner of the room, and she turned to discover Tommy had been listening. "That was quite a performance, Carolina."

She slid to the end of the piano bench, then swung around to face him. "Thank you. I think it helped."

Rising from his chair, Tommy joined her on the bench. "What's troubling you? That wrinkle on your brow is deeper than the Grand River!"

She told him of Joshua's proposal.

"Got your mind made up?"

"Almost," she replied, a rift of thirty-second notes playing unbidden in her mind.

Tommy took her small hand in his large, steady ones, a hint of clove drifting to her as he looked straight into her eyes with his calm, blue ones. "I think you'll make Mr. Joshua Bolden a fine wife."

Wife. She'd thought of herself as many things—student, musician, and more recently, teacher, but the wifely role had always seemed far in the future.

"Just think of all the duets you'll play," Tommy continued, "musical ones, parenting ones—"

"Children!" Caroline blurted out. Motherhood was another role she'd given little thought to.

Tommy laughed. "First you'll be a trio, then a quartet, maybe even a quintet some day."

"Oh, stop it!" she said with a smile, then she pulled her hands free to pace solo across the room. Staring out the window into the dark of night, she asked herself if she was really ready to accept Joshua's proposal. The apartment above the store sounded cozy. The name, "Mrs. Joshua Bolden," held great appeal. But as for the rest . . . her thoughts were interrupted by a tinkling on the keyboard, Tommy's one-finger rendition of *Here Comes the Bride.* Staccato laughter burst from her lips, reducing her anxieties to *pianissimo.*

"You don't give up, do you?" she accused, joining him once again on the piano bench.

He immediately started playing *Polly, Wolly, Doodle.* When they had finished the simple duet, he rose, saying, "Don't make things more complicated than they are, Carolina. If you love Joshua, marry him." And on that note, he headed upstairs.

The following morning, after a brief conversation with her mother, Caroline somehow managed to concentrate on music long enough to teach the two students scheduled for lessons. Afterward, she headed to Bolden & Sons Hardware, her feet carrying her swiftly along the walkway.

Joshua's heart played an erratic drumbeat the moment Caroline came through the door. Thankful that no customers were in the store at the moment, he crossed the wooden floor to greet her.

"Hello, Caroline."

Joshua's words and expression were both tentative. The shadow beneath his eyes attested to his lack of sleep, a condition Caroline was feeling keenly, herself. Offering a timid smile, she asked, "May I please speak with you in private?"

Giving a nod, Joshua led her to the back room, dreams of an acceptance to his proposal dying with every step. When his father and Zimri had passed through, carrying a walnut chest from the alley to the furniture showroom, Joshua pulled closed the curtain that separated the storage area from the front of the store and invited Caroline to take a seat on the shrouded chest that now seemed depleted of all hope.

Perching on the edge, Caroline leaned toward Joshua, seated on a stool in front of her, and reached for his hands. Her focus remained briefly on the work vest he wore. The word *Joshua* embroidered over his pocket had never looked quite so handsome as it did this day.

"Joshua," she began, her gaze rising to meet his, "I've

come to give you my answer."

His heart took a bar's rest, as did his breathing, so certain was he that Tommy had stolen her affections.

She spoke again, ending the agonizing silence. "I've come to tell you that I want to marry you!"

He tried to swallow. His throat wouldn't work. Nor would his tongue. But his hands automatically tightened around hers in a grip he couldn't control.

Caroline tried vainly to wiggle her fingers. "I'm afraid my piano-playing days will be over, if you don't loosen your hold on me," she gently chided.

He released her, his brain still in a fog of joyous disbelief. "You're going to marry me . . . you're going to . . . " In a single movement, he rose from his stool and pulled her up into his arms.

Laughing softly, Caroline declared, "I love you, Joshua Bolden! I love you!"

Joshua set her down, gazing into the most sparkling brown eyes he'd ever seen. Her smiling, heart-shaped mouth was irresistible in its appeal. "May I kiss you?"

She nodded, welcoming the gentle pressure of his lips against hers.

One kiss left Joshua eager for more, but he restrained himself, pulling her against him in an embrace that was reduced to hand-holding seconds later when Zimri came through the curtain.

In an instant, he sized up the situation. "Smiling faces. Must be a wedding in the offing." At Joshua's nod, he added, "Congratulations! Now, if you'll excuse me, Mr. Finkbeiner's come to pick up the tool kit he ordered last week." Reaching behind Joshua, he claimed the goods from the storage shelf and left them alone again.

131

Releasing her hands from Joshua's, Caroline pressed smooth her blouse and skirt, saying, "Mother and I are hoping you and your family are free to take dinner with us tonight. Is your mother home? I'd like to extend the invitation."

"Far as I know, she's home, and we're free," Joshua said, calculating the hours till he'd be with Caroline again.

Heading for the door to the alley, Caroline said, "I'll just slip out the back and go ask her. See you later, Joshua."

He walked her out, watching her until she'd crossed Mill Street, mounted the front porch, and been invited inside by his mother. On feet that barely touched the ground, he returned to the back room. Pulling the old sheet off the family heirloom hope chest, he ran his hand across its smooth surface, silently praying, *Thank you, Lord, for turning my hopes into reality!*

The balance of the day passed at *tempo allegro* for Caroline. Accompanying her mother to the Barber Meat Market, she chose a sizable cut of prime ribs for Vida to prepare. Afternoon hours were spent in the music room composing the first movement of a trumpet solo with organ accompaniment for Joshua. Inspiration flowed so rapidly through her mind and off the nib of her pen, that the piece practically wrote itself. With the solo and piano accompaniments complete, Caroline closed the keyboard cover to go upstairs and dress for dinner.

She chose the peach-colored lace garment she had worn at her graduation dinner, taking a moment to apply a small amount of the lip color Deborah had left behind. At the thought of her cousin, Caroline couldn't help wishing

Deborah were here to share in the happy occasion. Nor could she help wondering where and what the girl was doing now. Returning the lip color to Deborah's vanity, Caroline pressed such questions from her mind with a prayer that the Lord would look after her errant cousin and soon bring her back to Caledonia. At half-past seven, Caroline headed downstairs, meeting her father and Tommy on their way up to wash and change their shirt collars before the 7:45 dinner hour.

In the dining room, Caroline found the table attractively set with her mother's finest sterling and Wedgwood china. In the center, she had placed a crystal bowl filled with white tea roses from the garden. And around the base of each candle stick was a ring fashioned with more of the same. Her mother came up behind her, pens and place cards in hand. "I'm glad you're ready a few minutes early. I thought perhaps you'd like to make out the place cards for Joshua and Zimri."

"I'd be happy to," she replied, taking the pen and the two blank cards her mother offered. On Joshua's, she penned his name in calligraphy, then, in the corner, added two heart-shaped sixteenth notes whose stems were linked by a pair of arrows. Setting the cards in place, she went out onto the porch to watch for the arrival of the Bolden family. She had expected to find them walking down Lake Street. Much to her surprise, they came aboard the Bolden & Sons freight wagon, its bed laden with the same shrouded piece of furniture that had served as a seat for her in the back of the store earlier in the day. She hurried off the porch to meet them as Mr. Bolden pulled alongside the front walk.

Joshua, handsome as ever in his grey summer suit,

offered a grin as wide as Emmons Lake. "I've brought you a betrothal gift. Got a place inside where we can set it?"

CHAPTER

14

With the help of Tommy and her father, Caroline soon had the center table in the parlor moved aside to make room for Joshua's delivery. He and Zimri skillfully maneuvered it through the foyer and into the parlor, lowering it carefully to the flowered oriental carpet. Eager to take a look at the shrouded gift, Caroline reached for the old sheet, but Joshua stopped her, taking her hand in his.

"There's a story that goes with this," he explained. "Papa tells it best."

When all the Boldens had been properly greeted, everyone was seated in the parlor. Caroline and Joshua took the love seat, his father the balloon-back chair nearby. When Mr. Bolden had loosened the tie about his thick neck and dabbed perspiration from his wide forehead, he tucked his handkerchief into his pocket and began to speak.

"In the old country, 'way back in 1850, my grandpa had a habit of visitin' the *rathskeller*."

At Caroline's puzzled look, Joshua explained, "In Germany, there was usually a beer room and restaurant in the cellar of the town hall called a *rathskeller*."

Mr. Bolden continued. "Times were hard in the old country. My grandpa and his three friends would sit around a table in the *rathskeller*, each with a stein of beer, and dream about coming to America. But Grandpa and two of his friends were too poor to save money for passage. They worked at the local brewery and made only enough money to pay their bills, nothing more. But the third fellow—his name was Zimri—was a little better off.

"Zimri worked for the cabinetmaker. As time went by, he grew more and more skilled at his trade until he was nearly as good as the master cabinetmaker for whom he worked. Soon, customers started requesting Zimri's work. He would spend long hours making deeply carved headboards and footboards, tables and chairs. But he always took time at the end of the day to meet with his friends at the *rathskeller* and play a few hands of skat.

"One day, Zimri came in with a big smile on his face. When grandpa asked him why he was so happy, Zimri pulled a leather wallet from his pocket. Taking four tickets from it, he lay them on the table, saying, 'In six months' time, my *Frau* and I and our two sons will be leaving the fatherland forever. We're sailing to America!' Grandpa and his two friends were very happy for Zimri, and just a little bit jealous.

"Over the next several weeks, Zimri continued to work hard all day long, and visit the *rathskeller* in the evening. He often spoke of how lucky he was to be going to America and how much he wished his friends and their families could emigrate, too.

"But, as time passed, grandpa and the others noticed changes in Zimri. His face grew gaunt, his skin, ashen. Sometimes he didn't come to the *rathskeller* after work.

When Grandpa and the others inquired after Zimri's health, he said he was a little tired.

"Then, one month before Zimri and his family were to emigrate, he came into the *rathskeller*. He hadn't been there for almost three weeks, and his friends were very happy to see him. But Grandpa could tell that Zimri was even thinner and paler than before. And when he began to deal cards to Zimri for skat, Zimri put up his hands. 'I won't play skat tonight,' he told them, 'but the three of you must play.' Pulling his wallet from his pocket, he lay his four tickets to America on the table. 'My family and I are not going to America,' he explained, 'I am sick, and soon will die. But the winner of this hand of skat may have these tickets and take our place on the boat to America.'

"Grandpa immediately told Zimri, 'You must sell your tickets and give the money to your *Frau*. She will need it, if she is to be a widow, soon.' The other two agreed, urging Zimri to put his tickets away.

"But Zimri shook his head, saying, 'Life has been very good to me. I have provided my *Frau* and our *kinder* with all they need after I am gone. My *Frau* is the one who told me to give the tickets to one of my friends. But I cannot choose among you. Then God gave me the idea that you three should play a hand of skat to determine who will cross the ocean.'"

Hearing the story, Caroline began to understand how God's influence could be present where she least expected —in a card game. She listened eagerly while Mr. Bolden continued.

"Zimri dealt the cards to his friends, laying the two skat cards face down on the table as is done in this game. Bidding began. Back and forth, it went, until Grandpa was the successful bidder. He picked up the first of the two cards on the table. It was the jack of diamonds. Since he had several diamonds, he showed it to his opponents to establish trump. Then he picked up the second card and placed it in his hand.

"Grandpa discarded two cards and began to play. The game was close. All depended on the last trick. But Grandpa knew he could take it. He lay down the last card he had picked up from the table, the ace of diamonds, and the game was his."

Caroline turned to Joshua. "Is that the ace of diamonds you carry in your pocket?"

Joshua nodded.

"No wonder you treasure it," she said, praying he would some day regard it for what it was—a keepsake—rather than a good-luck charm.

Mr. Bolden continued his story. "Zimri gathered together the four tickets he had laid on the table and placed them in Grandpa's hand, saying. 'You must be at the dock in Hamburg in one month's time. Godspeed!'

"The next day, as Grandma was setting dinner on the table, a clatter arose outside the front door. When Grandpa went to see who was there, he discovered Zimri delivering a beautiful new chest with intricate carvings. He told Grandpa, 'This is the chest I made to carry my belongings to America. I want you to have it.'

"Grandpa thanked him and shook his hand, and that was the last time he saw Zimri. But the day before Grandpa and Grandma were to leave for Hamburg, Zimri's *Frau* paid them a visit. She told them, 'Zimri is very weak. He will not live much longer, but he wants you to have this.' From the pocket of her apron, she pulled two beautifully carved letters—a 'J' and a 'B'—explaining, 'These are the last two pieces Zimri carved before he took to his bed. Put them on your chest so all will know it belongs to Johann Bolden.'

"A tear formed in Grandpa's eye as he saw Zimri's *Frau* out the door. He was too upset to eat, thinking of the good luck that had come to him, and the bad times that had come to Zimri. Instead of returning to the dinner table, he took out his tools and affixed the initials to his chest, thinking the whole night long about how his future was soon to change for the better because of Zimri."

Caroline wanted to speak up about the Lord and His control which directs all things, making good luck but a faulty human description for blessings, but she bit her tongue.

Mr. Bolden continued. "But the crossing to America was a difficult one. My father was only ten years old, and his brother, Fritz, was only seven. They became very sick on the boat. Fritz died at sea. Grandpa was afraid my father would die, too. He and Grandma prayed day and night that Papa would recover, and soon the worst was past and he began to grow strong again.

"After several weeks on the ocean, they arrived in America, and two months later, made their way to Michigan. As time went by, the chest that Zimri had made was passed on to my father. He gave it to me, and I gave it to Joshua."

Mrs. Bolden spoke up. "Joshua spent hours and hours refinishing it."

Zimri said, "He started on it in March. That's when we knew he was really sweet on you, Caroline."

She looked at Joshua in surprise. Color rose in his

cheeks as he squeezed her hand and pulled her to her feet, drawing her to the shrouded gift. "For months now, I have been filling the chest with all my hopes and dreams for our future. Now, I give them to you."

Pausing beside it, her hand on the sheet, Caroline thought of the distance the chest had come, the lives that had been changed by the man who had made it, and the lives that would yet be touched by this solitary piece of furniture. *Thank you, Lord, for the blessing of this chest,* she silently prayed.

Slowly, she pulled the sheet away, revealing an oak and pine chest that had been finished with an orange-tinged stain and several coats of varnish. The initials, J.B., were fancily carved with delicate curlicues and serifs. "This is beautiful," she told Joshua. "I'm highly flattered to receive such a special gift. Thank you."

The sincerity in Caroline's voice, and in her smile of appreciation, made Joshua's heart soar as he lifted the lid of the chest, allowing the aroma of freshly-sanded cedar to escape.

Ottilia rose from her chair, joining Caroline to admire the gift and inhale deeply of the aromatic cedar. "One thing's certain. This chest will keep the moths away," she concluded.

Pushing up the oval glasses that seemed too small for her plump, round face, Mrs. Bolden said, "Joshua fitted that chest with a brand new cedar lining this winter."

Zimri chuckled. "Spent days on it. We were beginning to wonder if he'd ever get it done!"

Caroline turned to her brother-in-law-to-be. "Zimri, I hope you don't mind that Joshua has given me this family heirloom, especially since it was made by your namesake."

He shook his head. "It has Joshua's initials on it. You should have it. Besides, that isn't the only heirloom in the family. When the time comes, my bride-to-be will have her share."

Just then, Vida came to announce dinner. When a blessing had been asked and the prime ribs served, discussion ensued concerning a wedding date for the couple, Ottilia saying, "Caroline and I have checked the calendar, and come to the conclusion that the second of September seems appropriate—providing the apartment over the store will be ready by then."

Mr. Bolden nodded. "It'll be ready. That's nearly two months off—plenty of time for me and Joshua and Zimri to put in a one-bedroom apartment with a music studio." Caroline was about to speak when he continued, his gaze shifting from her mother to her. "Mrs. Bolden and I were thinking we'd give you and Joshua a new spinet piano for your wedding gift. It'd be near impossible to haul anything bigger up the steps to the second floor."

Caroline prayed for a measure of understanding amongst the Boldens before responding. "You're very kind to make such an offer, but I've been giving it much thought, and concluded that instead of a music studio in the apartment, you should put in a second bedroom." She rushed on, lest anyone jump to a wrong conclusion. "I'm really quite fond of the piano here. It was a birthday gift from Mother and Papa. I'd like to continue using it, and the music room for my studio, unless anyone objects."

Joshua appeared ready to mount an argument when his mother spoke up. "That sounds like a very practical decision, Caroline. Instead of a piano, we'll give you other furniture for your apartment—you pick it out. There are plenty of catalogs to choose from in the store, aren't there, Joshua?"

"I . . . " Joshua had imagined the sounds of Caroline and her students at a piano on the second floor, their notes filtering down to the store where he would hear them while at work each day. The comforting thought of having his wife only a staircase away was a difficult one to give up. " . . . I'm sure there are plenty of catalogs. I'll show them to Caroline tomorrow."

Beneath the table Caroline reached for Joshua's hand, thankful that their plans for the future were blending so harmoniously.

CHAPTER

15

Mr. and Mrs. Charles C. Chappell
request the honor of your presence
at the marriage of their daughter
Caroline
to
Mr. Joshua Johann Bolden
on Saturday, September the second
at two o'clock
Methodist Episcopal Church
Caledonia

At her father's desk in the library following Sunday morning's church service, Caroline set the invitation with the others she had hand-lettered to let the ink dry, pausing to reflect on all that had been accomplished in the ten days since Joshua and his family had come for dinner in honor of their betrothal. The very next day, her mother had taken her to the best seamstress in Caledonia Township to pick out a pattern and fabric for her wedding gown. From Meda Bergy's swatch book and pattern samples, she chose a pale peach silk mull to be fashioned into a gown with a fitted bodice, ruffled neckline, long, narrow sleeves, and a draped skirt caught up by creamy rosebuds. Her head-piece would consist of satin bows and more rosebuds affixed to a brimless peach silk hat.

Caroline chuckled to herself about the fuss her mother had made over the color of her gown.

"You simply *must* wear white for a church wedding. Tongues will wag. People will say you're not . . . *pure!*"

"Let them talk," Caroline had argued, reminding her mother that last year, the newspaper had reported that the Lehman girl had worn a fawn-colored wedding dress, and Lucy Jahnke had been married in pale blue.

Roxana's Matron of Honor gown would be of a similar but narrower design executed in a soft mint green mull. She had already come from Grand Rapids for measurements, and would return in a week for the first fitting.

Tommy's laughter, floating in from the porch, reminded Caroline of the changes in his life, as well. Having located an apartment in Grand Rapids near her father's law firm, he had moved out of Caledonia and into the heart of the city last week. The move seemed only to have sharpened his appreciation for home-cooked meals and the quiet of the village, for upon her mother's invitation, he had gladly returned to spend the weekend, and made no secret that he was eagerly anticipating Vida's Sunday dinner.

The aroma of pot roast simmering amidst onions, carrots, and potatoes, was beginning to make Caroline hungry. She tried not to think about it as she set pen to cardstock writing out an invitation to the reception.

Reception
immediately following
Two hundred five Railroad Street

R.s.v.p.

She leaned the card against a vase containing an ivory
rose and was reminded of her mother's schemes for the
bridal bouquet and floral decorations in both the church
and at the reception which would take place in the garden.
She had already solicited contributions from every gardener
in the village and drawn up elaborate plans for bridal arches
to embellish the church aisle down which Caroline would
proceed on her father's arm. In addition, the table bearing
the wedding cake and punch bowl would be embellished
with an appropriate centerpiece.

Writing out another invitation, Caroline paused after
penning Joshua's name. A refrain from the trumpet solo
she had recently composed played in her head. She smiled,
remembering the arguments her mother had mounted
against playing the piece prior to the wedding ceremony.
*It's a mistake to perform at your own wedding. You'll be
too preoccupied to concentrate on music!* But with
Joshua's support, Caroline's plan had prevailed, and the
solo which had become a celebration of their love for one
another would be performed a few minutes before Mrs.
Barber played the wedding march.

The only problem now was finding time to rehearse.
She'd seen little of Joshua these past ten days. He, along
with his father and brother, had been putting in every available spare minute on the apartment over Boldens' store.

She missed Joshua terribly and felt deeply the need to spend time with him in these last few weeks before their wedding. Yet she knew she must be patient and understanding and refrain from uttering any word of complaint over the lack of his company, accepting what time he could spare for rehearsals as time enough.

At the sound of Vida's announcement that dinner was served, Caroline gladly set pen and invitations aside to join the others in the dining room. Her father had said grace and Vida had served portions of pot roast all around when Ottilia's gaze settled on Caroline.

"I still think it's a mistake to play at your own wedding. Suppose Joshua has an attack of nerves? It can happen even to the most confident of grooms," she warned, her focus shifting to Caroline's father who winked in response.

Repressing an urge to argue, Caroline politely reminded her mother, "The music program is agreed upon and I don't wish to change it." A new thought coming to mind, she added, "Unless Deborah were to return home, in which case I would ask her to sing *Oh Promise Me* after Joshua finishes his solo."

Ottilia's hand flew to her forehead. "Deborah! I'd quite forgotten about her with Caroline's wedding springing up so suddenly." Gaze shifting to Tommy, she asked, "Weren't you going to contact the Cleveland Pinkertons several days ago?"

He nodded, ready to speak when she turned to her husband.

"Charles, those investigators have had more than enough time to locate Deborah. Why haven't they brought the girl home? Her reputation's probably sullied beyond repair by now!"

146

Tommy replied for him. "We've had two wires from the Cleveland agency since Independence Day. When they couldn't find anyone by the name of Taman in Cleveland, nor anyone who's connected with both the banking and theater businesses there, they asked for a photograph of Deborah. Mr. Kinsey made a copy of the one he'd taken and I sent it to them, but even so, the detectives are at a loss to say whether she's in the city. Make-up and costuming can greatly change the appearance of an actress who doesn't want to be found."

"Then I'll go to Cleveland myself!" Ottilia concluded. "I'd recognize Deborah, costume or no!"

Charles wagged a finger. "Now, dear, you have too much to do right here to leave town before Caroline's wedding, and you know it."

"*Someone's* got to go!" she insisted.

Tommy said, "I'll go." To Charles, he said, "That is, if you can spare me from the office for a few days."

Ottilia objected. "But you haven't seen her in years. Do you think you'd stand any better chance of finding her than the Pinkertons?"

Tommy smiled. "Mrs. Chappell, do you remember that loud, shrill whistle I used when we were neighbors and I wanted Caroline and Deborah to come outside?"

Ottilia grimaced. "How could I forget?"

"If I can get within a quarter mile of Deborah, she'll hear my whistle, and I'll find her."

Caroline spoke up. "And Tommy can take the picture of Deborah that sits on your dresser. With that, and his whistle, I'm sure he'll locate her!"

Charles tapped the table with his fist. "Settled! Tommy can take the 5:40 train east tomorrow morning.

He'll be in Cleveland by the next day, and God willing, he'll have Deborah home before the weekend."

Ottilia sighed. "I certainly hope so."

Another thought dawned on Caroline. "It sure would be nice if Deborah were here for the pioneer picnic. You're going, aren't you, Papa? Joshua said his father's planning to close the store and take a break from working on the apartment so his whole family can spend the day together at Campau Lake. He and Mrs. Bolden were hoping you and Mother would be there, too."

Charles scratched his chin. "When is the picnic?"

"A week from Wednesday."

Ottilia told Charles, "Do try to clear your calendar, dear. It would be a nice get-together for the two families before vows are spoken."

When Charles's expression remained pensive, Tommy asked, "Isn't that the picnic your attorney friends, Mr. Clapperton and Mr. Carmody, were urging you to attend?"

Breaking into a smile, Charles replied, "By gum, you're right! They're giving speeches that day. I suppose I'd better be there, or they'll be extra hard on me next time we meet in court!"

CHAPTER

16

As her father turned east onto Sixty-eighth Street, Caroline couldn't help thinking that the Lord surely had blessed the Thornapple Valley Pioneer Association with the best weather of the season for their annual picnic. The sun shone forth, radiating off emerald cornstalks decked with golden silk on one side of the road, while balmy breezes surged softly across amber acres on the other. Caroline hoped she would be blessed with equally pleasant conditions for her wedding another ten days hence.

Ten days!

The thought brought her up short. In some ways, her special day would be here too soon. At least, that's what her mother—already worn out from organizing the event— lamented every day, wondering regularly if Caroline's dress would be finished on time, the garden properly set up, and the church decorated in time. The apartment above Boldens' store hadn't escaped her scrutiny, either. When they'd last seen it, the bedroom walls were still unfinished and the bathroom plumbing only a figment of Joshua's imagination.

Her mother's anxieties were rubbing off, setting Caroline's stomach on edge at the very thought of all that must yet be accomplished. Bowing her head, she silently prayed, *Lord, give me the peace of knowing that everything is in your keeping, even the finest details of my wedding and the apartment.* A new calmness descended, allowing her to again enjoy the beauty of the day.

While Tommy and her father conversed in the front seat and her mother dozed off beside her in the rear, her thoughts strayed to another dilemma still unresolved. Tommy's trip to Cleveland had failed to locate her cousin, or any information about the theater and banking businesses supposedly owned by Neal Taman's father and uncle. It was as if they didn't exist, at least that's what the Pinkertons had concluded. No one in the city had ever heard of Neal Taman. And no Cleveland banker was involved in the theater business. Further complicating matters was the fact that neither the Pinkertons, nor anyone employed at the theaters had seen a young woman who looked like Deborah. Caroline could only conclude as her father did, that there was much more to the situation than it appeared on the surface.

The troubling thought was put from mind as her father turned off the road and onto the picnic grounds at Campau Lake. With two hours to go before the midday meal, there were already hundreds of teams of horses unhitched from their wagons and chomping on grass in the shade of a grove of maple trees. At the two-storey Apsey Pavilion which overlooked the small oval of water nestled in the pine woods, scores of people sat or stood on the long front porch renewing acquaintances and catching up on the news since the prior year's picnic. In the surrounding grove, thousands more had claimed picnic tables, or spread blankets beneath the trees. Caroline was wondering how she would manage to find Joshua and his family when he emerged from the crowd, directing her father to a good parking place for his buggy and helping him to unhitch the team. While they led the horses to the shady resting place, she, Tommy, and her mother joined the other Boldens at one of the two tables they had claimed early that morning and set end to end. Tommy fell into conversation with Zimri while she helped her mother spread their cloth across their table. She was smoothing it out when Tess Johnson came by with an elderly woman.

"Miss Chappell, this here's my granny from Middleville, Orpha Johnson. Granny, this here's my pie-anna teacher, Miss Caroline Chappell."

The broad, bonneted woman cradled Caroline's hand in hers. "Bless you, dear, teachin' my Tess, here, the pie-anna and askin' nothing in return. She can never say enough good about you."

Before Caroline could reply, Tess said, "Miss Chappell's gettin' married, come the end of next week."

"I know that!" her granny replied, tapping her walking stick on the ground in mild irritation. It was then that Caroline noticed the woman's name had been carved up the side of the walking stick, giving it a truly unique appearance. She was about to comment when the old woman continued.

"Tess reminds me about your weddin' at least a dozen times each Sunday when she comes to see me." With a gentle squeeze of Caroline's hand, she told her, "I wish you all the best in your marriage, my dear. And I thank you again for bein' so kind to my Tess."

Caroline returned the woman's affection. "It's my pleasure, Mrs. Johnson." Hands parting, she added, "Now, you and Tess enjoy your picnic!"

"And you, the same!" came Orpha's reply as she and Tess disappeared in the thick of the crowd near the pavilion.

For Caroline, the hours of having Joshua at her side were the most pleasurable since their betrothal, even if she did have to share his company with three thousand or so other picnickers. After a filling meal of Vida's ham sandwiches, potato salad, and orange cupcakes, they spread blankets on the ground near the speaker's stand and settled down along with their folks and Tommy to hear the program. After some initial disappointment over the absence of the association's president, Mr. Campau, who was too ill to attend, Mr. Clements, the vice president of nearby Ada township invited Reverend Moffit to open with prayer. The first speakers were Mr. Clapperton and Mr. Carmody, the attorneys Caroline's father knew from his law practice. Their stories of the olden days when Grand Rapids was little more than a criss-cross of muddy streets, charmed and delighted the audience. They were followed by Mrs. Saunders, a state lecturer for the Grange who continued to hold her listeners captive with reminiscences of life before the railroad, but the last speech was by far the most entertaining. It was delivered by Mr. Eardly of Cascade, who spoke humorously about his early courtship. His story soon brought Caroline and Joshua to laughter, her woodpeckerish staccato ringing above the chuckles and chortles of those nearby. His tale was so engaging, she couldn't understand why Tommy would get up and leave in the middle of it. Assuming he was answering a call from nature that couldn't wait, she returned her attention to Mr. Eardly, enjoying every word as his escapade unfolded.

Neal Taman had been aware of Caroline Chappell's presence almost from the moment she had arrived at the picnic, and had been keeping his distance so as not to ignite another outburst from that irritating mother of hers. But that odd laugh of Caroline's pulled him with a magnetic force he couldn't ignore, the sound compelling him to draw closer until he was within twenty yards of her blanket. Taking a deep breath, he rooted himself there, watching and listening from the back of the crowd. Then that blasted Rockwell fellow got up to visit the latrine. Determined to keep out of sight, Taman changed position, losing himself amongst the audience on the opposite side of the grove. Removing his jacket, he spread it on the ground and sat down, confident he'd gone undetected. Until the program ended a few minutes later and he rose to find Caroline's childhood friend staring him in the face.

"Mr. Taman, I'm surprised to see you here, although I suppose I shouldn't be. You have a habit of appearing when—and where—you're least expected."

Picking up his jacket, Taman slung it over his shoulder, then extended a hand. "I don't believe we've been formally introduced. You are . . . ?"

The fellow nearly crushed his hand, pumping it vigorously. "Thomas Rockwell, a friend of Caroline Chappell and her cousin, Deborah Dapprich."

"Nice to meet you. Now, if you'll excuse me . . . " He tried to extricate his hand, but the blasted fellow refused to release him.

"Not so fast, Mr. Taman. I'd like to know the whereabouts of Deborah Dapprich."

Keeping a smile in place, he replied pleasantly, "I haven't the slightest idea where the girl's gone. Now, I suggest you let go of my hand, sir. I have business to attend to." Free of the fellow's grip, he headed in the direction of the pavilion, certain he'd lost Rockwell in the thick crowd until he reached the porch steps. An iron grip on his forearm spun him face to face with the young man once more.

"You've had Deborah taken somewhere, and it wasn't Cleveland. Now where is she?" The tremor in Rockwell's steely words spoke volumes about his anger.

CHAPTER

17

Determined to remain pleasant, Taman replied amiably to the Rockwell fellow. "You won't get any answers from me as long as your hand is clamped onto my arm."

Reluctantly, Rockwell released him.

Stalling for time to think, Taman laid his jacket over the porch rail and brushed the wrinkles from his shirt sleeve, asking, "How do you know the girl isn't in Cleveland?"

"The Pinkertons—"

"There you have it! The Pinkertons didn't do their job right during the Civil War, and they're not doing it right, now." Hurrying up the steps, he made his way into the pavilion. Rockwell followed, his questions continuing even after Taman reached his room on the second floor and slammed the door in his face.

Rockwell pounded on it, shouting at him through the pine planks until management came upstairs and forcibly removed him.

Taman watched from his window. Two minutes later he saw Rockwell heading away from the pavilion, presumably to join the Chappells. At the thought of Caroline, warmth surged within. He desperately wanted another look at her before the day was done, but he dared not leave the pavilion.

On the grounds below, he caught sight of another young lady he recognized—Tess Johnson. His warmth chilled quickly, jealousy surging as he recalled the girl's words when he'd crossed her path earlier in the day.

"Did ya know Miss Chappell's gettin' married, come the end of next week?"

With clammy, trembling hands he turned from the window and reached for the jacket that should have been hanging on the straightback chair. Then he remembered that he'd left it on the porch rail. He lay down for a nap, certain it would still be there in a couple of hours, after the Chappells and other picnickers had headed for home.

Caroline wondered what was keeping Tommy. The Boldens had already packed up and headed for home, as had most of the other picnickers. Her father had hitched up the team, and she and her mother had taken their places in the buggy. But there they sat. Twenty minutes later, he finally climbed aboard, brow furrowed.

"Sorry to keep you all waiting. I ran into a little problem."

Charles chuckled. "What's the matter? Didn't Vida's potato salad set well?"

"I . . . I'm fine, now, thanks," came Tommy's hesitant reply.

The ride home passed quietly, everyone evidently talked out after the long day of renewing acquaintances. Caroline dozed on the back seat, her head against her mother's shoulder. An hour later, she awoke to the sound of her father's loud pronouncement.

"End of the line! Everybody off!"

When the buggy had been put away, they gathered around the dining table for a light supper of Vida's cold potato soup. While her mother, evidently revived by the restful ride home, shared news of cousins, aunts, and uncles who hadn't been seen since the recital two months earlier, Caroline couldn't help noticing that Tommy was quieter than she'd ever seen him, seemingly preoccupied as he slowly stirred his soup, tasting of it every now and then without enthusiasm.

"Are you sure you're feeling all right?" she asked him, thinking he might still be suffering from indigestion.

"Me?" he asked, forcing a smile, "I'm fine. I'm a tad worried about Joshua, though."

"Whatever for?" she asked innocently.

He grinned. "That fella's so doggone elated when he's with you, Carolina, I'm about convinced he'll expire of pure happiness a week after you're wed!"

"Tommy!" she scolded, her face burning as her father laughed uproariously.

The light moment passed quickly, however, and when her father excused himself from the table, his path to the porch for a cigar was detoured by Tommy's request to speak privately with him in the library.

Caroline wandered into the music room intending to play through the accompaniment to the new trumpet solo she'd composed, but found herself lingering outside the door separating it from the library, wishing she could hear what was being said on the opposite side. But the voices were low, the words muffled. Half-heartedly, she sat at the piano, playing softly, vaguely conscious of mother passing by the open door, embroidery in hand, on her way to the porch.

Caroline had been biding her time for half an hour when the library door finally opened. She rose from the piano to look for Tommy, and was met by her father instead. "Orange Blossom, would you please fetch your mother?" he asked, his brief smile belying the sober look in his eyes.

"Is Tommy sick?" she asked, trying to peer past her father's broad form. She caught only a glimpse of Tommy beside the desk, studying what appeared to be a calling card, before her father's hands on her shoulders turned her in the direction of the front porch.

"Tommy's fine. Now please send in your mother."

She did his bidding, planning to enter the library on her mother's heels when her father intervened. "This conversation isn't for your tender ears, Caroline. Don't you have some practicing to do?" He turned her in the direction of the piano with a nudge.

Resentfully, she returned to the piano to play the *Maple Leaf Rag*. But her performance was half-hearted, her mind preoccupied by unanswered questions. Never had she seen Tommy so quiet and introspective. She tried to imagine what could be the cause—what could be so serious that her father would prohibit her from knowing about it?

Closing the keyboard cover, she muttered, "I'm eighteen years old, soon to be a married woman. I have a right to know what's troubling my closest friend." Confident strides carried her to the library. She paused, hand on the knob, silently asking God's help with whatever the problem might be before bursting through the door.

"I want to know what this is all about, and I want to know now!" she announced, proceeding quickly across the room. But before she reached the desk, Tommy grabbed up a calling card and slid it into his rear pocket. She stood before him, hands on hips.

"Let me see that!"

His downcast gaze shifted to her father, who drew a tight breath. "Believe me, Caroline, you don't want to know what Tommy found out at the picnic today."

She was about to argue when her mother spoke up.

"Your father's right, dear. It doesn't directly affect you, and there's no point in taking on unnecessary worry with your wedding day so close at hand."

Jaw set, she spoke every word precisely. "I'm not moving until I see that card."

Her father sighed, finally telling Tommy, "Go ahead, show it to her."

Tommy remained stock still.

Caroline held out her hand, palm up. "You heard him, Tommy. Give me the card."

With great reluctance, he laid the chit in her hand.

She studied the print on the small ivory card. Black embossed lettering noted an unusual address. She read it out loud. "'One Xanadu Place, Buffalo, New York.' What's located there?"

Tommy made no reply, his blue eyes full of anguish.

Without knowing why, she turned the card over. The image staring up at her made her gasp, her heart stopping momentarily only to race on. "What a judy I've been," she murmured, lightheadedness causing her to sway.

Tommy sprang to his feet, his strong hands guiding her into his chair. "I'm so sorry, Carolina, so sorry," he mumbled.

Her mind momentarily fuzzy, she closed her eyes while drawing a deep breath, then stared again at the photograph on the card to make sure she hadn't imagined it. There could be no doubt the scantily clad young lady was her cousin, Deborah, dressed in a low-cut, lace-trimmed corset cover and frilly pantaloons, posing on a fainting couch so as to reveal her feminine assets to best advantage. Her mouth wore a heavy application of lip color, and was pursed in a kiss-like expression. But it couldn't hide the troubled look in her delicate eyes, the apprehension on her forehead, or the tenseness in her jaw. She'd clearly been forced into circumstances that were not of her own choosing.

Caroline's gaze shifted to Tommy. "Where did you find this?" Her voice barely exceeded a whisper.

"At the picnic, like your papa said," he replied.

"I know at the picnic, but where? How?"

Her father explained. "He came across Neal Taman shortly before we left for home."

"But—"

Her mother spoke up. "When he pressed Mr. Taman about Deborah, the rotten fellow slipped off to his room in the pavilion."

Tommy said, "I followed him up to the second floor and tried to make him talk to me, but management said I was upsetting the guests and insisted I leave. On my way out, I noticed a jacket Taman had left on the porch rail. I checked his pockets and that's when I found the card."

Caroline stared at the photo again, eyes misting at the thought of what her cousin must be going through.

Her father said, "Now that we know exactly where

Deborah is, Tommy's planning to go to Buffalo and bring her home."

Tommy said, "I'm leaving tonight—taking the 1:15 train east. I should have your cousin back in Caledonia well before your wedding."

Caroline reached for Tommy's hand, giving it a squeeze. "Getting Deborah back is the absolute best wedding gift you could possibly give me, Tommy."

He squeezed her hand in return. "Pray for me, Carolina. My task won't be easy."

CHAPTER

18

Only two days remained before Caroline's wedding, and as she packed some personal belongings from her dresser drawers, she reflected on her trip last night to the apartment above Boldens' store. When she arrived she had discovered that the kitchen had no sink or ice box, the bathroom had no tub, and the bedroom had no bed. She tried to take comfort in the fact that the sitting room was cozy and complete, with a small couch in mauve velvet, an overstuffed chair and footstool in chocolate brown, and a bent rocker of polished oak. In the corner beside the couch stood the two-drawer oak cabinet she'd admired several times in Boldens' store.

Laying an orange blossom sachet alongside the stockings and petticoats in her bag, she paused to inhale the pleasant scent, her gaze falling on the portrait of Joshua on her dresser. She chuckled to herself. No groom worth his salt would bring his bride home to an apartment without a bed. And Joshua's mother had promised that she would supervise the installation of the sink, ice box, and tub, guaranteeing that they would be ready before she and

Joshua returned from their wedding trip.

Her bag full, she closed it and latched it. As she carried it past Deborah's bed to set it by the door, she couldn't help wondering whether her cousin really would make it home in time for the wedding. A full week had passed since Tommy had left for Buffalo, but not one word had been forthcoming as to his progress there.

The thought was interrupted by the ringing of the telephone. Caroline hurried to the top of the stairs, thinking her father might call her down to speak with Joshua. When he didn't, she went back to packing, only to be summoned to the parlor a few minutes later.

Notes in hand, her father slid the pocket door closed, explaining, "I've just spoken to Billy White, the assistant agent at the depot. He rang up with a lengthy telegram message from Tommy."

Caroline and her mother spoke almost at once.

"Is he all right?"

"Has he found Deborah?"

With a gesture toward the couch, he waited for them to be seated, then sat in the chair alongside. "Tommy's fine. He has Deborah and they'll be here in time for the wedding on Saturday."

Caroline was instantly pleased, but the somber look on her father's face as he studied his notes gave her pause.

Her mother pressed the issue. "You should be smiling, Charles. What else do you have to tell us?"

He studied his notes a moment more before explaining, "Last night, the police shut down the 'resort' where Deborah and several other young ladies were being forced to entertain men against their will. They took two of Taman's associates into custody—a man and a woman—but they haven't been able to locate Taman. They aren't certain, but they think he may be operating houses of ill repute in other cities."

Caroline shuddered. The evil impostor who had enticed her cousin into vile circumstances with the promise of a career on the stage was still free to lure others. Silently, she thanked God that Tess Johnson had not fallen victim to a deceptive offer, and she asked Him to help the police catch up with Taman before other young ladies were duped.

Her mother spoke again. "At least we'll have Deborah home soon. I'll leave worry about Taman to the police. I'm sure he's several states away, by now."

Caroline grew pensive. "It's still hard to believe what's happened to Deborah. When she left here, she had such high hopes for the future."

Ottilia sighed. "No principled man will go near her, now. Her reputation's ruined, stained for life."

Charles raised a finger of caution. "Ottilia, dear, wouldn't you agree that the least said about her misfortune, the better?" Not waiting for a reply, he told Caroline, "It's good that you're planning to include her in your wedding party. The important thing is to go on in as normal a fashion as possible."

"Normal?" Ottilia challenged. "It will be impossible to pretend everything is normal, once word spreads. By Saturday afternoon, the entire village will know exactly what happened to Deborah."

Charles shook his head. "Billy assured me he'll keep the entire matter strictly between the two of us."

Ottilia's gaze narrowed. "Yes, well, if it were Mr. Carey making the promise, I could believe it, but Billy White is young, and susceptible to the prying and pestering of his peers, and I'm just not entirely convinced he'll manage to live up to such a promise."

Caroline rose. "If you'll excuse me, I think I'll take a bath and go to bed. I could use some extra rest after all the packing I've done today." She paused to kiss her mother and father good night.

Charles clasped her hand, gazing up into her face with a look she couldn't quite read.

"What is it, Papa? Did you have something more to tell us?"

"I was just thinking. With your wedding coming up the day after tomorrow, I'll only get one more good-night kiss from my little Orange Blossom."

"Two more," she said, kissing him again. "Good night, Papa, Mother."

"Good night, dear," they replied in unison.

Twenty-four hours later, Caroline sat on the garden bench with Joshua, thankful that this last day before her wedding had finally come to an end. Laying her head against his shoulder, she drew in the sweet essence of roses—more pungent now that dusk had settled in—and gazed up into the heavens where the first twinkling stars were beginning to make an appearance. Silently thanking God for the beauty and peace around her, she couldn't help thinking this moment was a touch of heaven in comparison to her experiences of the past twelve hours.

The morning had dawned warm and muggy, only to grow more difficult by the hour. Two of the ladies who had promised to provide roses for the bridal arches inside the church rang up to say their supply of buds had mysteriously disappeared overnight, plucked from the bushes outside their very windows. While her mother was at Mr. Beeler's drug store making calls to Grand Rapids florists on the only long-distance phone in the village, Vida discovered that the Co-operative Farmers Butter & Cheese Company had come up short on the amount of butter and eggs needed for the little fruit cakes she would bake and box for the guests to take home with them. Later, the tent company had nearly ruined two rose bushes when erecting the awnings, putting her already overwrought mother in a real frenzy.

But thankfully, the wedding rehearsal had gone smoothly. The trumpet solo Caroline had written for Joshua, and for which she played the organ accompaniment, sounded forth without a single missed note. Mrs. Barber's experience at timing the wedding march had put Caroline and her father at the altar precisely on cue. And Pastor Phillips's calm manner in leading everyone through the practice ceremony lent reassurances that all would go flawlessly tomorrow.

Caroline was glad that Joshua had resisted Zimri's invitation to celebrate his last night as a bachelor playing skat, choosing instead to spend time alone with her—a situation that had occurred all too infrequently since their betrothal.

Joshua released her hand to slip his arm about her shoulder. Tipping her chin, he gazed deep into her eyes, his mouth curving in a modest smile. "You're mighty quiet tonight."

She smiled up at him, encircling his neck with her arms. "I was just thinking about our wedding trip. A week from now, we'll probably have gotten our fill of each other's exclusive company, don't you agree?"

He kissed her lips briefly, her orange blossom essence enticing him to thoroughly cover her neck with more gentle kisses, but he restrained himself, replying candidly, "If we were to go away for a whole month, I wouldn't get my fill of being alone with you."

Her smile broadened, her reply coming in a half-whisper. "It's good to know I'll have a happy husband for at least a month."

"At least," he confirmed. Studying her brown eyes so free of guile, he couldn't help thinking how pure, innocent, and completely virtuous she was, and how eager he was to exchange the vows that would make her his mate for life.

But tomorrow was several hours away. Tonight, they both needed their rest. Rising from the bench, he pulled her up beside him and began walking her back to the house. "I want you to go straight up to bed and get a good night's rest. Tomorrow's too big a day to start out tired."

Caroline couldn't help smiling. Joshua was sounding like a husband already. And she couldn't argue with his advice.

As they reached the side steps to the porch, Joshua pulled her close for one final hug. When she pressed against him, he felt the lump in his pant pocket, suddenly remembering the little box he'd placed there before the wedding rehearsal. Pulling it out, he set it in Caroline's hand. "I almost forgot to give you your wedding gift."

She studied the velvet box with a look of true surprise. "How thoughtful! But I haven't anything—"

"Open it," he urged.

She lifted the lid to find a gold necklace. Its delicate chain held an orange blossom with a tiny diamond at its center. "It's truly lovely. Thank you, Joshua." She rose up to kiss his cheek, but wound up being kissed on the lips instead.

Joshua hadn't intended to kiss Caroline so thoroughly, but the longer the kiss went on, the tougher it was to pull himself away. Finally, he forced himself to part from her, turning abruptly to leave with a mumbled, "See you tomorrow."

"Tomorrow," she promised, still tingling from Joshua's kiss as she hurried up the porch steps and into the house.

From the cornfield behind the Chappell home, Neal Taman watched the betrothed couple, hoping Caroline would linger on the porch; cursing fate when she promptly headed inside. He was determined not to let the Bolden boy have her. Thoughts of Caroline Chappell standing with that fellow at the altar in church made his blood boil. He'd see to it they never got that far.

CHAPTER

19

Caroline slept soundly for a few hours, then tossed and turned, rising from bed before dawn. Pulling on slippers and a thin cotton wrapper over her dimity nightgown, she tip-toed down the hall so as not to wake Parker and Roxana in the next room. Passing her parents' partly opened door, she continued on down the stairs in search of cooler air. She was headed for the side door when she encountered Vida, already at her baking in the kitchen.

"Too early, you rise," she scolded, spatula wagging. "The bride should get more sleep."

"It's too hot to sleep," Caroline explained. "I'm going outside for some fresh air."

Despite the hired woman's frown, she stepped out onto the porch. The eastern horizon was dimly lit with the first peachy glow of dawn. Descending the steps, she crossed the side yard and entered the awning in the garden. A scent came to her—a sickeningly sweet one she'd smelled before, but it wasn't from a flower she recognized. She was trying to remember where she'd come across such a perfume when she heard her mother's voice calling from the porch.

"Caroline?"

"Here, Mother, in the garden."

The words had barely escaped her mouth when a vile-smelling cloth smothered her and her world went black.

Joshua had slept only in fits, waking well before the first light of dawn to lie awake in bed. He was too full of nervous anticipation to fall asleep again, and too tired to get up. But when the telephone rang, he bolted out of bed to answer it, shocked by the panicky sound of Mrs. Chappell's voice.

"Joshua, Caroline's been kidnapped! It's that Taman fellow! I saw him! He just . . . "

Joshua could hear Mrs. Chappell collapsing in hysteria, then the calmer voice of Mr. Chappell.

"Son, Caroline's missing. She went out into the garden a few minutes ago. When my wife went out after her, she saw this Taman fellow drag Caroline off to a wagon and drive away. I've called the constable."

Joshua's heart raced, fury raging within. "I'll be right over."

Bolting up the stairs, Joshua roused his brother and father, the three of them arriving at the Chappell home a few minutes later. Vida met them at the front door, directing them to the library where Mr. Chappell, Parker, and the village constable, Abram Konkle, were already in discussion.

The constable, badge prominent on his too-tight vest,

apprised them of his plan. "We've got to take the fastest horses in the village and cover every route leaving town."

Charles explained further. "Taman headed east on Railroad Street. From there, it's anyone's guess which direction he turned. I'll take Cherry Valley north."

Joshua spoke up. "I'll take it south."

Mr. Bolden said, "I'll take Hundredth Street East."

The constable turned to Zimri. "If you'll go with me over to Whitneyville Road, we could split up—one going north, the other, south."

Zimri nodded.

Parker said, "I'll stay here. Goodness knows, Mother needs someone to calm her nerves."

The constable nodded. "Now, for horses. The livery's got some saddle horses that are real spry, but they require a firm hand on the reins."

Charles said, "I've got two swift, but gentle mares in the barn—one for myself and one to spare. Who wants her?"

Mr. Bolden said, "I do. I haven't kept saddle horses in years—only my draft team." To his sons, he said, "You fellas go on over to the livery with the constable."

Joshua matched Zimri and the lawman's swift pace for Daklin's Livery, behind the hotel, eager to get on Taman's track as quickly as possible. He was wishing they had more clues as to where Taman might have taken Caroline when the hefty livery proprietor revealed some interesting answers to the constable's probing questions.

"Yeah, that Taman fellow was in a couple days ago for my small wagon—the one with the built-in storage box beneath the bench. Told me he was driving over to Byron Center—even asked directions. But Mr. Finkbeiner came in shortly after and mentioned he'd passed the same wagon headed south on Cherry Valley. Didn't add up—'less that Taman's got a real faulty sense of direction." He laughed heartily.

The constable said, "We'll have both routes covered, once we get saddled up. Give us your fastest mounts."

Daklin pointed out two geldings and a mare. With four pair of hands pitching in, Joshua, Zimri, and the constable were soon mounted. Adjusting his battered felt hat to better shade his eyes, Konkle gave last minute instructions.

"Don't be afraid to knock on some doors and ask folks if they've seen a wagon the likes of Daklin's. And be careful. This Taman fella's unpredictable."

Joshua's hand automatically went to his pocket. Rubbing the tattered ace of diamonds between his fingers, he silently prayed, *Lord, help us find Caroline, and keep us all safe!*

Taman snapped the reins against the back of the mare he'd rented and cracked his whip, eager to cover as much road as possible before full daylight. With a mile behind him, he had five more to go before he could remove his precious cargo from the feather-padded bed of the wagon and secret her away in the apartment he'd let. Then, he'd simply have to wait for the ether to wear off before he could thoroughly enjoy her. The thought sent a burning warmth through him, stirring longings he'd denied himself again and again over the two-and-a-half months since he'd first encountered Caroline Chappell.

He cracked his whip, sending the mare into a burst of speed. The wagon shook, jostled by a bumpy stretch of road. He was silently berating the livery proprietor for overly-stiff springs when the right front wheel hit a hole and flew off, rolling into the ditch alongside the road.

He pulled up hard, coming to a halt. Climbing down, he retrieved the errant wheel, leaned it against the wagon, and gazed down the road. The rooflines of a house and barn were discernible in the gray of early morning. A dim yellow glow lit the barn window, and he headed there on foot, ready to handsomely reward the farmer for his aid. At the end of the driveway which must have been a quarter mile long, he noticed the name "Brogan" on the mail box. Moments later, he stepped through the open door of the barn and called to the elderly, skinny fellow who was shoveling manure into a bucket.

"Mr. Brogan?"

He squinted at Taman, set down his shovel and came toward him. "Do I know you?"

Taman shook his head. "Lost a wheel off my wagon half a mile from here. Can you lend a hand? I'm in a bit of a hurry." He flashed a twenty-dollar gold piece.

Brogan smiled, pocketing the coin. "You just bought yourself the best repair service this end of the county. Now show me that broken down wagon."

Ten minutes later, Taman watched and listened while Brogan inspected the wagon. "Hub of the wheel needs some work. Won't take much to fix it, but that axle . . . " He scratched his chin and shook his head. "Better bring 'er to my barn." He began rolling the loose wheel along the drive.

Taman followed, leading the horse and wagon toward the barn, casting backward glances now and then at the tarp-covered cargo on the wagon bed, watching for signs of movement. But his captive didn't stir. In the barn, Brogan immediately went to work on the wagon wheel. He'd been at his task for only a few minutes when a woman—evidently his wife—appeared in the doorway, apron filled with fresh eggs.

"Breakfast 'll be on soon as I fry up your eggs. Better get washed up." To Taman, she said, "You stayin' to breakfast, young man?"

Brogan answered for him. "Better put a couple extra eggs in the pan for Mr. . . . never did get your name."

Taman answered readily, "Hill. Horace Hill." To the woman, he said, "No need to trouble yourself, ma'am. I'll just wait here while you folks eat."

Brogan shook his head. "You'll eat with us, Mr. Hill. It's gonna be awhile 'fore you're on your way again."

Taman followed him to the well pump where they shared soap and a towel. Gray light of dawn now revealed a couple dozen cows in a pasture, the ribbon of road that stretched between Caledonia and Middleville, and the approach of a swift rider from the north who slowed up to turn down the Brogans' drive.

Taman's heart raced. Even in the dim light and from a distance, he sensed that it could be one of the Boldens in search of Caroline. Pulling out a five-dollar gold piece, he held it in Brogan's face. "If anyone asks, you haven't seen me."

Brogan tucked the coin into his pocket, head dipping in agreement.

Taman beat a swift pace for the barn, concealing himself behind the partly open door where he listened to the words being spoken a few feet away.

"Mr. Brogan, did you see anyone drive by here in a small wagon this morning?"

174

The voice was Joshua's, and Taman held his breath while Brogan answered.

"Ain't seen no passers-by."

The sound of hooves heading back down the driveway faded, then Brogan came into the barn. "I spoke the truth. You didn't pass by. Now we'd best get to the breakfast table, or my wife 'll be in a snit."

Caroline stirred, her mind in a dense fog, her nostrils filled with the unmistakable odor of a barn. She opened her eyes to the darkness of a shroud that completely covered her. In the distance, cows mooed. Feebly, she attempted to push the stiff canvas away, but it wouldn't budge. She closed her eyes again, too groggy to puzzle out where she was, or even what day it was. Giving in to the overwhelming need for more rest, she snuggled deeper into the feather bed upon which she lay and allowed slumber to claim her.

She wasn't sure how much time had passed when she opened her eyes again. No longer was she surrounded by darkness. Instead, she lay in a huge, frame bed in the center of a dim room. Her mind in confusion, she tried to find something she recognized, only to discover a vaguely familiar form bending near her.

"You're finally waking up, I see." The warm, velvet-toned voice was accompanied by the pleasant scent of roses, and a more pungent, sweet smell—one she'd smelled before, but couldn't seem to remember where. Nor could she quite place the narrow face, thin lips, and tenuous smile of the doctor-like fellow looking down on her.

Her mind moving slower than *adagissimo* and blanker than a clean sheet of staff paper, she gave up trying to remember who this fellow was, turning away as she mumbled, "Go away and let me sleep."

Sliding back into her slumberous haze, she felt his hand upon her shoulder, his warm breath upon her cheek as he whispered in her ear, "Sleep on, Miss Chappell. Sleep on . . ."

When her eyes next opened, the fellow was sitting in a chair to the right of the bed, polishing a small pistol as casually as if it were his pocket watch. Bit by bit, she remembered a past encounter with this man at the Independence Day Celebration. She had even danced with him. The sickeningly sweet scent was that of his hair tonic—unlike any other.

But why was she with him now? Cognizant thought drifted off, and returned with the image of her cousin's lovely face. Deborah had liked this man. Then Deborah had run away.

All at once, all too clearly, she remembered who he was. Neal Taman! The one who had lured her cousin away and forced her into a life of shame! Other faces and memories crowded in.

Joshua!

Caroline sat up with a start, her eyes wide open. "What day is this?"

At the sound of her voice, Taman slipped his gun inside his coat, a wicked smile gracing his mouth. "My sleeping beauty awakes. Can I get you—"

"Answer me!" she demanded.

He drew a breath. "It's the second of September."

"My wedding day!"

"You didn't really think I'd let that Bolden fellow have you, did you?" he asked cynically.

His features softening, he continued. "I've long had

176

plans to make you mine. *I* will be the one to take away your innocence. But not yet. For a few more hours, we'll stay in Middle—right where we are, then we'll move on, and I'll take you for my bride, have my way with you."

So they were in Middleville, only six miles from home. She took comfort in such knowledge, and the claim that she hadn't been taken advantage of her in her drugged stupor. But the possibility of becoming his unwilling bride set her in motion. She threw off the covers, then clutched the sheet to her when she discovered she was clad in nothing more than her dimity nightgown. Locating her wrapper at the end of the bed, she pulled it on, her goal the door. But the moment her feet met the floor, Taman rose, his pistol in her face.

"Sit down, Miss Chappell!"

His countenance, dark and angry, caused her to shrink back, sinking into the edge of the mattress.

"Now, *stay* put, or I'll tie you down."

"But . . . I need to visit the washroom," she claimed, fussing with the ring on her little finger.

He sighed. "It's across the hall." Beckoning with a flick of his gun, he unchained and opened the bedroom door.

She stood to follow, nearly falling when she discovered that her balance was still a bit off. His arm went firmly around her waist, guiding her into the hallway.

Directly opposite the bedroom, a washroom door stood open. To the left was a set of stairs, leading Caroline to conclude she was on the second floor. But that was her only observation before Taman walked her to the closet-like bathroom and pulled the string on the light.

"Don't try anything foolish. I'll give you two minutes,

then I'm coming in." He released her and closed the door to wait in the hall.

The room was windowless. There was no hope of escape—not even a chance to sneak a message to someone below. And if she were to scream for help, there was no telling what harm Taman might do to her. She availed herself of the facility, tightening the belt on her wrapper then pulling the chain on the water tank. At the sound of the toilet flushing, Taman opened the door, guiding her back to the bedroom with a solid grip on her elbow.

While he was closing and chaining the door, she perused a shelf holding a vase of white roses and half a dozen books. "Since we're going to be here for a while, I think I'll read," she said sweetly, pulling a Bible and a volume of poems from the meager collection. Propping pillows against the headboard, she fussed for several moments trying to find some means of escape while Taman stood and watched. Seeing no way out, she finally sat down and leaned back against the feathery support. He returned to his chair and his gun-polishing.

It was then that she noticed several more bouquets of white roses—on the oak vanity against the left wall, on the mahogany bed stand to her right, and on a round, cloth-covered table by the room's only window—a window which leaked bright daylight past its closed blind. She reached for a rose from the vase to her right, inhaling its perfume. The scent brought the Caledonia rose theft to mind. She leaned forward, a question slipping off her tongue before she could stop it.

"Did these roses come from Caledonia?" Immediately, she regretted the words, and her accusatory tone.

"So what if they did?" Taman snapped, gun waving.

Twisting the ring on her little finger, she smiled tentatively. "They're lovely—so lovely I thought at first they must have come from my neighbor's prize rose bush, but," studying the rose further, she added, "I can see now that these roses are even finer than the ones I was thinking of. You probably paid a florist a fortune for them."

He laughed and put away his gun, tenderness returning. "White roses you wanted on your wedding day, and white roses you got."

The thought of Taman as her husband made her feel sick to her stomach. Her heart ached for Joshua, and she wanted to cry out for him, but neither sentimentality nor hysteria would get her out of this fix.

"What time is it, Mr. Taman?" she asked, wondering how many hours until darkness.

He consulted his pocket watch, his mouth curving in a sardonic smile. "Half past two. The church is full of guests who know by now that the bride isn't going to show up for her own wedding."

Caroline couldn't deny that he was probably right. She could only hoped that the guests were all praying for her safe return, which gave rise to another question. She posed it cautiously.

"Mr. Taman, you say we're going to stay here for a while, but I can't help wondering . . . then where will we go?"

He offered a kind smile. "I thought I might take you to see your cousin. How would you like to go to Buffalo?"

"Buffalo?" she pondered out loud, "On the evening train?"

He shook his head. "On the night express—half-past one in the morning."

"I suppose I can be ready by then," she joked lamely, praying that she would find an exit from Middleville and Taman long before the train's departure.

He laughed and went to a wardrobe in the corner of the room where he pulled out a plain grey cloak and a white silk dress. It was fancy enough to be a wedding dress with its lace bodice, high ruched collar, and narrow, ruffled sleeves. "Later on, you can get into these. But for now, you might as well rest." He hung the garments on the wardrobe door and came over to sit on the bed beside her. Caressing her cheek with the back of his hand, he gazed into her eyes with his icy blue ones, his voice a ragged whisper. "You don't know how long I've dreamed of this day, Miss Chappell. For weeks— months—since our very first meeting on the fifteenth of June, I've tried to forget you. But no matter how far I traveled or how hard I worked, your dark eyes, your chattering laugh, your magnificent musical talent haunted me." He leaned closer, his hand trembling as he turned her chin to kiss her cheek.

A chill ran up Caroline's spine. She wanted to push him away, free herself from his touch, but she dared not anger him.

Abruptly, he rose, wandering off to the window, his back to her as he peered past the blind to the scene below.

She picked up the Bible and shrank back against the feather pillows. She *must* get away from Neal Taman before the night express rolled into town. Opening to Psalms, her mind was in turmoil. She closed her eyes and prayed that the Lord would quell her panic. When she opened them again, they focused on these words in the thirty-second chapter. *I will instruct thee and teach thee in the way which thou shalt go: I will guide thee with mine eye.*

Silently, she prayed again. *Heavenly Father, instruct me now in the way which I must go in order to part from Mr. Taman's company.*

Providentially, her stomach growled and sharp hunger pangs followed, along with an unquestionable desire for orange gum drops and a new idea. Hoping to convince him to make an extended visit to the candy store, she spoke deferentially.

"Mr. Taman, I really hate to bother you, but I have an insatiable craving for gum drops—lots and lots of them—and only the orange ones."

He turned from the window to offer a puzzled look.

She rattled on. "In Caledonia, I used to go over to Mr. Kinsey's general store and pick out the orange ones from his jar. I'd stand there and pick and pick until I had a nice fat bag of them. Then Mr. Kinsey would weight them up and I'd go home and make an entire meal of them," she exaggerated. "I'm hoping you'll go out to the store and pick me a bagful of orange gum drops because I doubt I'll be able to think of anything else until I get them."

"Orange gumdrops?" he asked, pondering the odd request. "Perhaps what you need is a nice steak. The landlady here will be glad to fry one up—"

"No!" She shook her head vigorously. "Orange gum drops are what I need." Slipping out the side of the bed away from the door so as not to alarm him, she began pacing the floor. "Orange gum drops, orange gum drops. It's all I can think of. I can almost taste them!" Gazing directly into her captor's puzzled blue eyes, she said, "*Please*, Mr. Taman, get me a nice plump bag of orange gum drops before I absolutely go out of my mind!"

"All right, I'll get them," he offered, "but only if you promise to get back into bed and stay put."

"Of course!" she agreed, hopping beneath the sheets.

He unchained the door and stepped out, locking it behind him. Instantly, she was out of bed, peering through the keyhole. But Taman didn't leave the hall. Instead, she heard him call loudly for a Mrs. Johnson, then watched and listened as slow, heavy footsteps approached.

Much to Caroline's astonishment, it was Tess's granny who appeared. She recognized the woman's heavy form and her fancy walking stick—the one with her name carved up the side. How Caroline wanted to cry out—to explain that Taman was holding her captive! But she dared not make a sound, for Taman was holding his pistol in the woman's face. She listened to his instructions.

"I want you to go to the confectionery shop across the street and get me a bag of orange gum drops—only the orange ones, mind you." He wagged his pistol for emphasis. "And remember, not a word of me to anyone else. I'll be watching from the window, and if everything doesn't go perfect, I'll see to it you never lay eyes on that granddaughter of yours again."

Tess's granny wiped tears from her cheek with a trembling hand. "I . . . I won't say nothin'. Please don't take my Tess. *Please!*"

Nudging her forcefully toward the stairs, Taman warned, "Mind what I say!"

When he inserted the key into the door again, Caroline dove onto the bed, getting between the sheets in a nick of time.

Taman commented as he chained the door and headed for the window. "Your gum drops will be delivered in a few minutes. Be patient, Miss Chappell, and try to think of something else, like your cousin, and the wedding you and I will have when we arrive in Detroit."

Caroline's stomach again in knots, she prayed it would settle enough to keep down the candy she had so boldly requested.

Hot, tired, and discouraged, Joshua and Zimri entered the Cobb & Scott store in downtown Middleville to the congenial greeting of the owner, Lavern Cobb, whose name was embroidered neatly on his white apron.

"Good afternoon, gentlemen! What can I do for you, this fine day?"

Mopping perspiration from his brow, Zimri stepped up to the counter. "Two things. First, lemon ices for me and my brother."

Reaching for tall glasses, Mr. Cobb said, "And . . . ?"

Joshua spoke up. "Information on the whereabouts of a fellow named Taman. We think he's somewhere in Middleville. Seen any strangers lately?"

Zimri added, "He's tall, with a narrow face, blue eyes, a neatly-dressed fellow."

Sipping from the lemon ice Cobb handed him, Joshua added, "He's driving a rig from Mr. Daklin's livery in Caledonia—a small wagon with a built-in chest beneath the driver's bench."

Cobb's brow narrowed in thought. "Several strangers have stopped by this week. Our reputation for fine confections has spread all the way to Battle Creek." He indicated the fine assortment of hard candies, nuts, taffy, and licorice in the row of glass jars in front of the counter. "Can't say as I remember a fellow by that description, though, or a

wagon like the one . . . " He paused to scratched his temple.
"Wait a minute. Now that you mention it, I believe I *did*
see such a rig pull 'round back of The St. James this
morning." He indicated the hotel across the street.

Joshua shook his head. "We've been over there.
Didn't see a wagon anywhere near it like Daklin's."

Cobb said, "Unless it's parked inside one of the barns in
the neighborhood."

Zimri shrugged. "I suppose it could be hid."

Joshua's gaze narrowed on his brother. "Maybe we'd
better take another look."

Zimri swallowed the last of his lemon ice and plunked
his glass on the counter. "Soon as I get a refill—and a bag
of hard candies. It's been a long, dusty day."

As they finished their second round of lemon ice,
Joshua and Zimri explained the separate trails they'd been
on since early morning—investigations which had brought
them together and sometimes sent them in circles, finally
leading them to downtown Middleville where their hopes
now lay of finding the man who'd abducted Caroline.

Emptying his glass for the second time, Zimri told
Joshua, "Like you said, we'd better take another look. And
maybe have a talk with the folks at the St. James."

Joshua nodded, and was heading for the door when it
opened to admit a plump, bonneted woman.

Cobb greeted her heartily. "Good day, Mrs. Johnson!
How's business at the St. James? Keeping those rooms
clean, are you?"

"Good day, Mr. Cobb," came the brief, subdued reply.

Despite the bonnet brim which hid much of the customer's face, Joshua could see that she looked anxious. Her
cane beat a rapid rhythm as she headed straight for the jar

of gum drops. "Come in for some gum drops. Got a bag handy?"

Cobb opened a small, white paper sack and offered it to her. "These fellows are trying to track down a small wagon with a chest built in beneath the seat. I told them I thought I'd seen one pull 'round behind the hotel this morning. Know anything about it?"

Joshua watched as Mrs. Johnson ignored the candy scoop and proceeded to pick only the orange gum drops from the jar, hands trembling. With a quick shake of her head, she told Cobb, "Ain't seen a wagon the likes of that."

Joshua stepped closer. "Mrs. Johnson, have you seen a fellow in town—tall, narrow face, neatly dressed? Goes by the name of Taman."

A gum drop fell from her unsteady hand. "I ain't seen no fella such as you describe." To Mr. Cobb, she said, "If you'll just weigh these up, I gotta git back."

As she reached out to hand the bag to Cobb, Joshua intercepted, grabbing hold of it to shake it in front of her nose. "Who's this for, Mrs. Johnson? Who wants only the orange gum drops?"

CHAPTER

20

Agitated, Taman stood by the window, watching through a narrow slit in the blind. "Something's gone wrong," he muttered to himself. "It's taking too long. That blasted woman's talking—I just know it!"

Fearful for Mrs. Johnson and eager to calm him, Caroline spoke in the most soothing tone she could muster. "It takes a long time to pick out enough orange gum drops to fill a bag. I've been known to spend an entire half hour at it."

He half-acknowledged the words with a dark glance her way, then peeked past the blind again, a cynical smile spreading slowly across his face. "Here she comes. Alone, too." Heading for the door, he listened for the unmistakable sound of Orpha's cane in the hallway, then unchained the door and stepped outside.

Again, Caroline listened and watched through the keyhole as Taman took possession of the bag, opening it to inspect. "Well done, Mrs. Johnson. You did just as I told you. Now go on down to the kitchen and tell the cook I want a big, juicy steak, a mound of mashed potatoes, and a generous slice of apple pie. And deliver it to me at half past five."

"Yes, sir," she replied, cane clunking as she headed for the stairs.

Again, Caroline hopped back into bed just as the door swung open.

Mouth twisting with a prideful smile, Taman presented her the white paper bag. "There you are, Miss Chappell. Gum drops—just the orange ones—exactly as you requested."

"Thank you," she replied, wasting no time in popping one into her mouth. Despite her lack of hunger, the orange flavor had a soothing effect on her as she chewed the sweet, gummy confection.

Evidently at ease with the latest mission accomplished, Taman sat in the chair by her bed and leaned back, eyes drifting shut before he opened them with a start, yawned, and slapped himself on the cheek.

Caroline could see now the dark circles of exhaustion beneath his lower lids, and prayed that he would allow himself to fall asleep as she quietly chewed one after another of the orange candies. It seemed her prayer was being answered when his eyes drifted shut a second time.

Reaching for another gum drop, she was pondering how she would divest Taman of his weapon and his key when her fingers came into contact with something thin and stiff at the bottom of the paper bag. Peering inside, she stifled a gasped at the sight of a dog-eared playing card—Joshua's ace of diamonds!

Her response was enough to interrupt Taman's nap. Waking with a start, he clutched his gun, pointing first at her, then the door. "What is it?"

"I . . . uh . . . nothing, Mr. Taman. I just realized I'd already eaten almost all of the gum drops. I didn't mean to startle you."

He stood and approached her, staring at the limp bag as if debating whether to take it from her. She prayed he would not, God granting her desire when Taman extended his hand, palm up, and asked politely, "Miss Chappell, may I have one of those gum drops, please?"

"Certainly," she replied, pulling three from the bag and placing them in his hand.

He popped them into his mouth and returned to the window where he stood silently, staring down on the scene below.

Slipping her hand back into the bag, Caroline clutched the ace of diamonds, rubbing it between her fingers as her silent plea went up. *Dear Lord, thank you for letting me know Joshua is near. Please help him find a way to bring me to safety. In Jesus' precious name, Amen.*

Finishing the last of her candy, she surreptitiously slipped the ace of diamonds into her wrapper pocket, then put aside the empty bag and opened up the Bible. While Taman kept his vigil by the window, she passed a long while reading and praying, taking comfort in the words of Peter. *For the eyes of the Lord are over the righteous, and his ears are open unto their prayers: but the face of the Lord is against them that do evil.*

She wanted to share the scripture with Taman, tell him the good news of Christ, that He forgives, and saves, and blesses those who love Him. But a small, still voice within warned her that this was not the time. Taman had hardened his heart against God, and to speak of Him now would only anger the man and put her in greater danger.

Her throat constricted, a tear welling up at the sad thought that Taman had slipped from grace and condemned himself to a never ending death. She prayed for his salvation, that by some means, he would come to know and serve Jesus.

Returning to the Bible, she resumed her reading until the tap of Mrs. Johnson's cane sounded in the hallway, her voice penetrating the thick oak door. "Dinner's here, sir."

Gun in one hand, Taman unchained and unlocked the door with the other. But the instant he turned the knob, the door burst open, smashing him in the face.

Taman fell back, hitting the side of the bed and slumping to the floor.

Joshua pounced on him.

Gunfire rent the air.

Joshua knocked Taman's pistol loose, sending it skidding across the floor.

While Taman struggled against him, Caroline scrambled off he bed to claim the gun. No sooner had she retrieved it than Zimri and Samuel Carlisle, the white-bearded village marshal, barged in, helping Joshua subdue Taman. They turned him face down, the marshal locking his wrists in handcuffs behind his back.

Not a second later, Joshua's arms were around Caroline, crushing her against him. "Thank God, I found you!" His voice was husky with emotion. A moment later, he pulled back, his worried blue eyes searching hers. "If that scoundrel violated you, so help me, I'll—"

"You needn't worry," she hastened to assure him, "He kissed me on the cheek once, but that's all."

As Zimri and the marshal hauled Taman to his feet, the lawman told him, "Looks like you're gonna be spendin' some time in a room decorated with steel bars."

Taman made no reply, his head hanging low as the marshal escorted him from the room.

Releasing herself from Joshua, Caroline hurried into the hall. "If you don't mind, Mr. Carlisle, I'd like to have a word with Mr. Taman before you take him away."

The marshal turned Taman toward her with a jerk. "Be my guest, miss. Tell him what's on your mind. He can't hurt you, now."

Though Taman refused to look at her, she quietly told him, "I'll be praying for you, that you'll ask God to forgive your wickedness, and that you'll come to know the grace and peace of Jesus Christ."

With a thud-thud-thud, Orpha Johnson emerged from the shadows in the hall, rapping Taman on the leg with her cane. "You'd better do as Miss Chappell says. 'Cause if ya don't, y'r gonna find yourself in a mighty hot place!"

Taman kept his silence.

When the marshal had hauled him away, Mrs. Johnson took Caroline's hand in hers. "Miss Chappell, I sure am sorry for all the trouble. I didn't have no idea Taman 'd taken someone to his room. Onliest thing I know'd was that he hauled up a big muslin sack this mornin' 'bout ten o'clock. Turns out, you were inside it!"

Joshua came beside Caroline, slipping the grey cloak from the wardrobe about her shoulders, and his arm around her waist. "Zimri and I had tracked Taman to Middleville and were in Cobb & Scott's confectionery across the street trying to figure just where in the town he'd hid, when Mrs. Johnson came in and started picking out the orange gum drops. That's when I found out exactly where you were."

Reaching into her pocket, Caroline produced Joshua's

tattered ace of diamonds. "God works in mysterious ways His wonders to perform."

Joshua smiled. Sliding the old playing card into his own pocket, he bent to kiss Caroline, his intentions of a brief kiss extending to a more prolonged contact which ended at the sound of a distant train whistle.

Zimri spoke up. "That's the 5:43 express. If I ring up the agent and tell him what's happened, he'll stop the train for us and we can be back in Caledonia by six o'clock. The entire village is waiting for Caroline's return, by now."

Wondering out loud, Caroline said, "Do you suppose there's any chance we could still—"

Joshua answered before she finished, his arm tightly about her as he guided her through the hall toward the stairs. "I'm taking you home, and I'm gonna to marry you before anyone can stop me!"

On the train ride to Caledonia, Caroline thanked God that her future with Joshua was back on track and destined to become the perfect duet.

Historical Notes

Some street names in the story, taken from a 1907 map of the Village of Caledonia, differ from those in use today. Main Street was called Center Street, and Kinsey Street was called Railroad Street. None were called "avenues."

Many business names mentioned in the story are historically accurate, but Bolden & Sons Hardware and Furniture is fictional. The Wilson family, real-life occupants of the the fictional heroine's home during the early 1900s, were owners of the Caledonia Farmer's Elevator.

Interior descriptions of buildings in the story are completely fictional.

About the Author

Donna Winters moved from New York State to Grand Rapids, Michigan in 1971, and from Grand Rapids to Caledonia, in June 1977. Her first published romance was released in 1985, and several more have followed.

She has lived all of her life near the Great Lakes. Her familiarity and fascination with these remarkable inland waters and her residence in the heart of Great Lakes Country make her the perfect candidate for writing *Great Lakes Romances*.

Caledonia Then and Now

Where have all the churches gone?

The following pages offer a glimpse of four churches from Caledonia's past. Facing each historic photo is a contemporary scene showing current use of the same site.

The Methodists sold their Main Street property to a congregation of Baptists, built a new United Methodist Church on Vine Street, and celebrated the first service there on Easter Sunday, 1963. The Baptists eventually relocated. The old church was torn down in the late 1970's, its timbers rising again in the form of a storage barn. An Ameritech facility now occupies the original site of the church.

The Liberal United Brethren Church, dedicated in 1900, ceased to exist during the first half of the 1900's. Its site became the location of a private residence which was left to the Methodist Church and served as its parsonage from 1966-1980. Today, the home serves as a private residence.

The Caledonia Evangelical Church on Short Street was built in 1885, and when no longer needed by its congregation, served as a basketball hall and later as a storage building. It was torn down in 1974 and replaced by a new Caledonia Lumber Yard storage facility.

The only church structure still in existence of the four pictured is the former United Brethren Church on Emmons. This building became the Caledonia Library in 1981.

Several new, larger churches have sprung up in the Caledonia area over the years, serving the spiritual needs of the community in much the same way as the old, smaller structures once did.

Methodist Church
Main Street at Church

Main Street at Church

Liberal United Brethren Church
Main Street at Maple

Main Street at Maple

Caledonia Evangelical Church, *Short Street*

Short Street

United Brethren Church
Emmons Street at Church

Emmons Street at Church

Caledonia News

In researching Caledonia's history, many interesting items from the village newspaper, *The Caledonia News*, came to light. The most fascinating of them follow.

April 8, 1904, front page
Traffic in Girls.
Immense Demi-Monde District to be Established at World's Fair.
Handed in for publication.

"A certain rich syndicate has entered into a contract with the world's fair commissioners under which it is granted the privilege of erecting certain buildings near the entrance to the exposition grounds. These buildings are now in process of erection. They are large massive structures and are to all outward appearances hotels, lodginghouses and similar places for the entertainment of visitors to the world's fair. Now mark the conditions of the contract. In order to secure these concessions the syndicate agrees first to pay the world's commission a stipulated sum of money; second, to provide 2500 innocent girls to be used for the gratification of the brutal passion of the devils in human form who are capable of taking advantage of such a condition! Note the adjective, innocent girls. How are innocent girls to be obtained? There can be but one way. It means that they are to be kidnapped, and these buildings are being constructed and arranged with that special purpose in view.

"These facts have been published and hinted at, but what is being done? The world holds its breath in horror when the news of the awful disaster in the Chicago theatre was flashed around the globe, but calmly contemplates the fact that 2500 pure girls are to be torn from their homes, outraged, ruined, lost body and soul. Think of it father, mothers, you who have beautiful daughters of your own, think of it Christian people; think of it, ministers of Christ's gospels, you who from your pulpits have access to the ears of millions; think of it, men of the press, you who send your messages wherever man is found; think of it, every man and woman in whose breast beats a heart to be stirred by such a tale of horror; think of it, and then arise in the power and righteous indignation and declare that while God reigns this hell-born contract shall never be fulfilled."

--Happy Homes.

June 9, 1905
16 Graduate This Year
Commencement Exercises June 23
Baccalaureate June 18 at M.E. Church
On Friday, June 23, at 7:30 p.m. the Caledonia high school will graduate one of the largest classes in its history. The class of '05 is composed as follows:

Roy D.White
Anna Vollweiler
Sadie McCullough
Solon E. Winter
Louretta Adams
Edward Petted
I. Ellen Kriedler
Arthur Sherk
Gordon Bergy
F. Pearl Colby
Frank Loring

Edna Amon

Blaine McWhinney

M. Jane Wenger

Carrie Deifenbaker

Mary Wenger

The commencement exercises will be held on Friday, June 23, commencing at 7:30 p.m., at the M.E. church. Following the custom of last year, an admission of 10 cents will be charged.

The baccalaureate sermon will be given by Rev. J.G. Phillips from the pulpit of the M.E. church Sunday, June 18, at 7:30 p.m.

August 6, 1904

Dr. D.M. Johnson, a recent graduate of a Buffalo school, has been in the village the past six weeks soliciting life insurance. He owes a large board bill at the hotel and Wednesday night after some trouble with Landlord Cavanaugh it is alleged that he attempted to leave on the midnight train. He was prevented from doing so; a rig was procured and he was invited (?) to get in and was taken to Grand Rapids accompanied by H.B. Cavanaugh, W.D. Kennedy, Chas. Forward and Ray Glowczynski, where he was arrested charged with attempting to jump a board bill. Further particulars we cannot give this week, but it is said that he will fight the case. Johnson owes a livery bill of about $30, also other smaller accounts and some borrowed money. About a week ago a party in the village received a letter from a party in Hastings putting the people next to his game. It is alleged that he owes twelve different people at Hastings in sums ranging from eighty cents to $15. He was well liked by his acquaintances here and helped the local doctors in several difficult cases. He is a young man and weighs about 250 pounds.

Editorial Note: The following three items, all appearing in the August 26, 1904 newspaper, raise an interesting question about a certain culprit in the village.

While Mr. and Mrs. Jacob Fulwiler were attending the Wm. Blake funeral last Monday someone entered and ransacked the house from top to bottom and secured only about $1.25 in money. Nothing else was missed. Luckily, Mr. Fulwiler put $500 in his pocket that he had in the house. No clue.

F.M. Barber, proprietor of a meat market here, went to Grand Rapids Monday where he swore out a warrant for the arrest of Roy Cook, his clerk, on a charge of till tapping. The warrant was served Tuesday and he was taken to Grand Rapids by Constable Charles Timm where he had a hearing before Justice Granger. He pled not guilty and the trial was set for next Wednesday. Jacob Fulwiler, his father-in-law, went his bail in the sum of $200.

Notice.
To all whom this may concern:
I emphatically deny any charge F. M. Barber has made against me. I am guiltless of any crime whatever as the proceedings will show.
Yours respectfully
Roy Cook
"One of his clerks."

August 26, 1904 cont.

The population of the village of Caledonia according to the census just completed is 569 as compared with 427 in 1900 which represents a gain of 33-1/3 per cent. This is an exceptionally large gain and is the highest of any village in the county. There has been a large number of dwellings erected in the village the past year; many more would find ready renters.

Population of Middleville in 1900 was 829 but now it is 831.

April 28, 1905

Lots of women would like to stay at home and look after the children and the house, but if they did their friends would say their husbands were brutes.

June 16, 1905

While loading a barrel of salt back of the elevator Wednesday, George Schiefla's team became frightened at a train and ran around onto Main Street where they ran into Ben Glick's buggy and nearly demolished it. One horse fell down and they were caught.

June 23, 1905

A reception was given Wednesday evening by Mr. and Mrs. L.T. Herman at their home in honor of the class of "Naughty Five." The rooms were beautifully decorated, the library with palms and roses, the dining room with the class colors in bunting, and laurel twined around the pillars in the hall and sitting room. A sumptuous supper was served in courses at 6 p.m., at which was presented to each member of the class the class flower and souvenir. The evening was spent with music and entertainment provided for the occasion, after which all departed for their homes, having enjoyed the evening immensely.

September 8, 1905
A Fierce Fight

A fierce, bloody fight took place in the village Monday evening, the principals being Edward Converse and Charlie Forward of Alaska.

The affair started over a game of cards in Fry's saloon where the contestants held a slight "brush." Later, it was renewed in front of Wenger & Cook's market and the combatants fought desperately. Forward enjoyed a nice "chop" steak from Converse's face and the latter seemed to be satisfied with "thumb" steak.

When Constable Konkle attempted to arrest them Jay Hoover interfered and they came together again. Converse went to Grand Rapids Tuesday, pleaded guilty and paid his fine. Deputy Kennedy came out Tuesday and together with John Spaulding took Forward to the city and he also paid the fine and costs. Mr. Hoover also paid a fine for interfering with an officer.

Fights are getting altogether too frequent in the village of late. A few arrests accompanied by stiff fines might tend to put a quietus upon them.

More *Great Lakes Romances*
For prices and availability, contact:
Bigwater Publishing
P.O. Box 177
Caledonia, MI 49316

Mackinac First in the series of *Great Lakes Romances* (Set at Grand Hotel, Mackinac Island, 1895)

The Captain and the Widow Second in the series of *Great Lakes Romances* (Set in Chicago, South Haven, and Mackinac Island, 1897)

Sweethearts of Sleeping Bear Bay Third in the series of *Great Lakes Romances* (Set in the Sleeping Bear Dune region of northern Michigan, 1898)

Charlotte of South Manitou Island Fourth in the series of *Great Lakes Romances* (Set on South Manitou Island, Michigan, 1891-1898)

Aurora of North Manitou Island Fifth in the series of *Great Lakes Romances* (Set on North Manitou Island, Michigan, 1898-1899)

Bridget of Cat's Head Point Sixth in the series of *Great Lakes Romances* (Set in Traverse City and the Leelanau Peninsula of Michigan, 1899-1900)

Rosalie of Grand Traverse Bay Seventh in the series of *Great Lakes Romances* (Set in Traverse City, Michigan, and Winston-Salem, North Carolina, 1900)

Jenny of L'Anse Bay Special Edition in the series of *Great Lakes Romances* (Set in the Keweenaw Peninsula of Upper Michigan in 1867)

Elizabeth of Saginaw Bay Pioneer Edition in the series of *Great Lakes Romances* (Set in the Saginaw Valley of Michigan, 1837)

Sweet Clover: A Romance of the White City, Centennial Edition in the series of *Great Lakes Romances* (Set in Chicago at the World's Columbian Exposition of 1893)

Isabelle's Inning Encore Edition in the series of *Great Lakes Romances* (Set in the heart of Great Lakes Country, 1903)

Also by Bigwater Publishing
Bigwater Classics
Thirty-Three Years Among the Indians
The Story of Mary Sagatoo
Edited by Donna Winters

In 1863, a young woman in Massachusetts promised to marry a Chippewa Indian from the Saginaw Valley of Michigan. He was a minister whose mission was to bring Christianity to his people in the tiny Indian village of Saganing. Though he later became afflicted with consumption and learned he hadn't long to live, his betrothed would not release him from his promise of marriage. Soon after the newlyweds arrived in Michigan, this Chippewa Indian extracted a deathbed promise from his new wife.

"Mary . . . will you stay with my people, take my place among them, and try to do for them what I would have done if God had spared my life?" Joseph asked, caressing her hand.

"Oh, Joseph, don't leave me," she begged, *"it is so lonesome here!"*

"Please make the promise and I shall die happier. Jesus will help you keep it," he said with shortened breath.

Seeing the look of earnestness in Joseph's dark eyes, Mary replied, "I will do as you wish."

Thus began a remarkable woman's thirty-three years among a people about which she knew nothing—years of struggle, hardship, humor, and joy.

READER SURVEY—*Unlikely Duet*

Your opinion counts! Please fill out and mail this form to:
Reader Survey
Bigwater Publishing
P.O. Box 177
Caledonia, MI 49316

Your
Name:_____

Street:_____

City,State,Zip:_____

In return for your completed survey, we will send you a bookmark and the latest issue of our *Great Lakes Romances Newsletter*. If your name is not currently on our mailing list, we will also include four note papers and envelopes of an historic Great Lakes scene (while supplies last).

1. Please rate the following elements from A (excellent) to E (poor).

_____Heroine   _____Hero   _____Setting   _____Plot

Comments:_____

_____

2. What setting (time and place) would you like to see in a future book?

_____

(Survey questions continue on next page.)

3. Where did you purchase this book? (If you borrowed it from a library, please give the name of the library.)

_____

4. What influenced your decision to read this book?

_____Front Cover _____First Page _____Back Cover Copy

_____Author _____Title _____Friends

_____Publicity (Please describe)_____

_____

5. Please indicate your age range:

_____Under 18 _____25-34 _____46-55

_____18-24 _____35-45 _____Over 55

If desired, include additional comments below.